"Did you talk to the kids this morning?"

"They weren't up when I left for work."

Leigh did her best to shut down the mental image he'd just given her. Her daughter in bed with his son, the two of them cuddled up together like...lovers.

She closed her eyes and tried to replace that picture with another—the path she'd jogged along that morning. Feeling slightly calmer, she said, "Well, they should be up by now. I think I'll head over to see."

"Okay. I guess I'll see you there."

"You go home for lunch?" Why couldn't he just bring a sandwich to work like most of the American workforce? She didn't want him present when she was talking to Taylor. Didn't want him watching. Interfering.

"I'm not the enemy, Leigh. I'm after the same thing you are. All I want is for my kid to be happy."

Happy, sure. But what about responsible? Considerate? Mature? Leigh didn't say anything, not wanting to start another disagreement.

Leigh to____ her b____th, then restarted her car. ____ ____ ____ sided overnig____ ____ was about to get a

Dear Reader,

You are about to read a love story about two single parents, both struggling—in their own ways—with children who are growing up and leaving the "nest." This is a difficult stage for all parents, but especially so, I think, for single parents. One of the ways Leigh Hartwell decides to cope is by training to run a marathon.

Are you someone who has caught the running bug? Every year hundreds of thousands of people run a marathon. That's a lot of people. And twenty-six point two miles is a lot of grueling foot pounding. For years I've been struggling with much more modest goals. I've worked my way up to hour-long runs several times a week. For me, that's enough. But many of my friends are much more accomplished and I'd like to thank Mike, Simon, Gloria and Janet for allowing me to experience the thrills and the pain of a marathon through their stories. Which really is the best way for those of us who would rather be turning the pages of a good book...

I hope you enjoy Leigh and Sam's story as they struggle to adjust to their "empty nest" and find love in the second stage of their adult lives. If you would like to write or send e-mail (perhaps share a running experience?) I would be delighted to hear from you through my Web site at www.cjcarmichael.com. You can also contact me by regular mail at #1754-246 Stewart Green S.W., Calgary, Alberta T3H 3C8, Canada.

Happy reading!

C.J. Carmichael

STAR-CROSSED
PARENTS
C.J. Carmichael

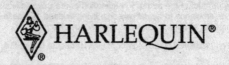

TORONTO • NEW YORK • LONDON
AMSTERDAM • PARIS • SYDNEY • HAMBURG
STOCKHOLM • ATHENS • TOKYO • MILAN • MADRID
PRAGUE • WARSAW • BUDAPEST • AUCKLAND

ISBN-13: 978-0-373-71429-2
ISBN-10:   0-373-71429-7

STAR-CROSSED PARENTS

www.eHarlequin.com

Printed in U.S.A.

ABOUT THE AUTHOR

Hard to imagine a more glamorous life than being an accountant, isn't it? Still, C.J. Carmichael gave up the thrills of income tax forms and double entry bookkeeping when she sold her first book in 1998. She has now written over twenty novels for Harlequin Books and strongly suggests you look elsewhere for financial planning advice.

Books by C.J. Carmichael

For M.N.F.
The book has already been written...

Thanks to the following wonderful people for helping me with my research: Mike Fitzpatrick, Simon Batcup, Gloria Fournier (all marathoners), Dr. Shouresh Charkhandeh, Dr. Gordon Bird and Gwen at Jefferson Inn

CHAPTER ONE

THE NOTE WAS STUCK to the fridge with a magnet when Leigh Hartwell came home from work, but she was too rushed to read it.

She set the bag of groceries on the counter, then opened the fridge to store the assorted cheeses she'd picked up for the party tonight. She'd hardly finished when the phone rang. It was the caterer, her friend, Tina O'Dell.

Leigh had a premonition of trouble. "Don't tell me you couldn't find fresh scallops."

"I found them." Tina sounded grumpy. "But why didn't you tell me you weren't inviting men to this party?"

"I sent you the guest list a month ago and you're just noticing that now? Anyway, why should it matter whether there are men at the party or not?"

It wasn't as if she and Taylor had set out to avoid them. It just so happened that when they'd listed the important people in their lives—her coworkers at the dental clinic and the people in her running group, Taylor's best friend and her pals from ballet—no males had made the cut.

"I bought a low-cut blouse to wear tonight, that's why it matters. I was going to look *hot*."

"I'll take a photo. You can put it up on an Internet dating site."

"Hey, I'm not that desperate. You, on the other hand—"

"No lectures, Tina. I don't have time." She still had to shower and change before Tina arrived with the food. "You still planning to be here in an hour?"

"Of course. I'm never late for a catering gig. So how was the run? You know I love Taylor and wouldn't have missed cooking for her party, but I hated to miss it."

"I didn't go, either."

"Leigh—"

"How could I, when I'm expecting twenty guests less than two hours from now?"

"But running relaxes you, and worrying about your guests is *my* job. If you trusted me—"

"I do. Really. I know everything will be perfect. It's just—what's one run? We'll both go a few extra miles on the weekend."

"This isn't about your training schedule. It's about your need to relax and enjoy yourself now and then. I want you to have fun at Taylor's party. Not worry about every little detail. Speaking of Taylor, how's our girl doing?"

"Actually...I'm not sure. She should have been home by now. There's a note on the fridge. Let me just grab it." She snatched it too quickly, sending the magnet flying to the floor.

"Wasn't today the first day of her new summer job?"

Leigh grabbed the magnet and stuffed it into the drawer where she kept pens and paper. "Yes, if she made it on time. She didn't get to bed until after midnight last night." She'd been on the computer again. Since receiving her letter of acceptance from Cornell University a month ago, Taylor was forever on their Web site.

"Look, Tina, I'd better run. See you soon, okay?" As Leigh returned the phone to the counter, she skimmed the note.

Hi, Mom, Taylor had written. *I know this is going to sound crazy...*

Leigh stopped breathing as she read the rest.

No. Impossible.

This had to be her daughter's sick idea of a joke.

She set the paper down, pulled out an open bottle of white wine and poured herself a glass. She took a long swallow, then read the note again.

I know this is going to sound crazy, Mom, but I've been chatting with this really nice guy over the Internet for several months and last week he asked me to come and visit him. Don't worry, he's a great person and I'm not in any danger. I'll call you once I get there.
Love, Taylor
P.S. Sorry about the party…

No matter how many times Leigh read the note, the message wouldn't change. And yet she still couldn't believe it. She and Taylor had had so many conversations about the dangers of meeting people over the Internet and the folly of dating someone you only knew through correspondence.

All those late nights when Leigh had assumed Taylor was either studying or researching Cornell…she'd really been chatting with this guy.

And who was he? Taylor had left her no clue. No name, no address, no contact information of any kind. Leigh grabbed the phone again and tried her daughter's cell phone. She was shuffled straight to the message service.

"It's Mom, Taylor. I've found your note. Please call me as soon as you get this."

Damn.

How could Taylor have done this? Leigh's daughter was a shy girl who didn't date much. Years of struggling with acne had left her self-esteem a little battered where boys were concerned. In a way, Leigh could understand why Taylor had felt more comfortable meeting a guy at the distance the Internet offered.

But why hadn't Taylor said anything? Their relationship was close, or so Leigh had thought, but she'd had no *clue* Taylor was carrying on this way.

Who was this guy? How old was he? Was he a predator?

No, no, don't panic. Stay calm. Think. Focus.

It was no use. One scary possibility led straight to another. Where was her daughter, right now? Still en route? Or had they already made contact?

The very idea had Leigh hyperventilating. *Don't worry,* the note had said. *He's a really nice guy.*

Well, how would Taylor know? Had she had the guy checked out? Leigh knew she hadn't.

Oh, God. Please don't let this guy be some sort of pervert.

Leigh jerked away from the table. The first thing she had to do was phone Kerry. Surely Taylor's best friend would know all about this.

But Kerry didn't.

"That's insane, Ms. Hartwell. Are you sure?"

Leigh read her the note.

"Taylor never mentioned a word about this guy."

"So you can't give me a name? You don't have any idea where he might live?"

"Sorry, I don't have a clue."

Leigh could have banged her head against the wall. "I can't believe Taylor would do something like this."

"I can't, either. It's totally not like her."

Leigh disconnected the call, more concerned than ever. For a moment she contemplated the bizarre possibility that her daughter had been abducted and forced to compose the note. But there was no sign of any stress in Taylor's neat printing. No sign of a struggle in the pristine apartment.

She checked her daughter's room and found it atypically neat. Taylor's backpack, the one she'd used for school, was missing. So were several pairs of jeans and her favorite hoodie.

Leigh looked in her own room next and found

her closet in disarray. Not a good sign. It was usually when Taylor wanted to look older that she borrowed from her mother's wardrobe.

The computer was the next logical place to go. Leigh and Taylor shared the same password, since it was a family machine, and she had no trouble getting into Taylor's e-mail account, though it was something she'd never done before.

She groaned at the list of saved messages, almost all of them from someone who called himself PartyMan. Why hadn't she thought to check up on her daughter sooner? The media were always warning parents to monitor their children's computer usage.

But Leigh never thought to worry about Taylor. She was such a good kid and there'd been no decline in her marks at school. Wasn't that one of the warning signs that were supposed to alert parents that their kid might be in danger?

But she couldn't pinpoint any changes in Taylor's demeanor or behavior. If anything, Taylor had seemed in higher spirits and even more cooperative these past few weeks. Leigh had attributed this to excitement about her graduation from high school and acceptance at Cornell. Apparently, though, her daughter had been excited about something else, entirely…

An Internet romance.

But was that really what was happening here? Fear crawled over Leigh's skin and she tried not to think of the many newspaper articles and made-for-TV movies about far more sinister scenarios.

Her daughter had a golden future before her. She had to be all right. She just *had* to be.

Leigh opened the most recent message from PartyMan and skimmed the contents. Most of the message contained plans for when he and Taylor would finally be together. It all sounded quite innocent…long walks together, picnics, listening to music, that sort of thing. But of course, if this guy was a pervert he wouldn't be broadcasting his intentions, would he?

Her attention zeroed in on the last paragraph of his message: *I'll pick you up at the bus station. It's just a few miles from my place. Can't wait to finally meet you!*

Her stomach dipped, and her skin crawled again. "I'll just bet you can't wait to meet her, you creep."

Needing specific details about their plans, she opened the previous message. It was all there. PartyMan's real name was Josh Wallace—or so he claimed—and he lived in a town called Jefferson in Mount Washington Valley, New Hampshire. He'd given Taylor information on the bus route, and, thank goodness, a home address.

Leigh closed the computer and picked up the phone again. She had to rent a car and go after Taylor right away. She was negotiating a weekly rate, with unlimited mileage, when the doorbell buzzed.

"Okay, that sounds fine. Can you have someone drive the car to this address?" She recited her apartment number and street quickly, as she crossed the room to the front door.

Tina O'Dell, her curly hair in a messy ponytail, arms laden with a huge casserole dish, stepped into the room.

"Party time," she announced gaily.

Leigh disconnected the call and shook her head. "Afraid not."

"What—"

"Taylor is missing and I'm on my way to find her. But first I'm going to call the police."

THE WINDOW of the 2003 Buick LeSabre slid downward and a grizzled face peered out from the driver's seat. "Fill 'er up, Sam."

Sam Wallace heard the phrase every day, and each time it made him smile. "Fill 'er up," sounded a lot like "Batter up" to him. Not too many people would see much in the way of similarities between playing baseball and working at a small-town gas station, but Sam did.

Though he hadn't played the game, or even checked a box score, in six years, baseball was part of him. He couldn't shake it.

"You bet, Ernie." He reached in the open window to clasp the older man's shoulder, before moving to the other side of the vehicle. He unscrewed the gas cap, then inserted the nozzle for regular unleaded gasoline.

He listened to Ernie chat about the Red Sox until the pump shut off automatically. He recapped the tank, then waited while Ernie counted out the twenties with age-worn hands. "Bloody oil companies," the older man muttered.

"I'll be right back with the change." Sam took the money inside to his nephew, Robin, who was working for him for the summer.

Two elderly women were sitting in chairs, waiting for the bus for Concord, which was due any minute. He nodded at them, then passed Robin the money. The sixteen-year-old passed him back the change with practiced efficiency.

While Sam was settling up with Ernie, the bus from Concord pulled in. Three young people emerged into the warm New Hampshire sunshine. He nodded at two teenage boys he recognized. They were often in the store buying slushy drinks and chatting up girls.

The young woman, though, Sam didn't think he'd seen before. He guessed she came from the city. She looked like a model, all made up with stylish clothes. But the expression on her face was that of someone young and vulnerable.

"You okay?" he asked. "You seem a little lost."

Her smile was sweet. "I'm fine, thank you. It's just that someone was supposed to meet me."

Her voice confirmed it. This was a New York City gal. He wondered what she was doing here, who'd she'd come to meet.

"Do you know Josh Wallace?"

Sam blinked. "Ah…sure. He's my—"

Before he could finish, the sound of squealing tires had both him and the girl turning to watch as Josh's van pulled into the station. Josh swung into a vacant parking spot, and a second later leapt from the driver's seat and jogged over toward them.

"Sorry I'm late." Josh sounded breathless and he looked…different.

Sam checked the impulse to comment on his son's reckless driving. He couldn't remember when he'd last seen that look in Josh's eyes. The girl seemed equally excited to see him, too. They couldn't take their eyes off each other.

He stepped between them and held out his hand to the newcomer. "I'm Sam Wallace, Josh's father."

"Oh." She shook his hand. "I'm Taylor Hartwell. It's nice to meet you, Mr. Wallace." She frowned. "You look kind of familiar. Are you—"

"Taylor's here to visit for a few days," Josh explained. He'd interrupted Taylor, but she didn't seem to mind.

"Oh?" Sam said. "You didn't mention anything at dinner last night."

Josh just shrugged, then hooked a hand around the straps of the backpack on Taylor's shoulders.

"Can I carry this for you?" he offered gallantly.

Sam struggled not to smile as Taylor slipped off the pack and passed it over. As he took a closer look at the girl, though, Sam felt a twinge of concern. "So, where are you from, Taylor?"

"New York City."

As he'd thought. "That's quite a distance from here. Where did you two meet?"

His stomach dropped when he saw the look that passed between her and Josh. At first it didn't seem as if they were going to answer his question. "Josh?" he prodded gently.

"On the Internet. A few months ago." His son squared his shoulders, unconsciously taking a stance that told Sam he was expecting criticism and was prepared to do battle against it.

It's a new world out there, Sam told himself. He'd seen plenty of articles in the paper about Internet dating sites and such things becoming more popular. No sense overreacting.

And yet…was the girl as old as she looked?

"Your family knows you're here?"

She nodded.

"Cut it with the questions, Dad." Josh sounded annoyed. "We've got to get going." Josh had slung Taylor's pack on one shoulder. With his free arm he took her hand.

"See you later."

Taylor twisted to face him, even as Josh pulled her toward his waiting van. "Nice to meet you, Mr. Wallace."

Polite girl. But she sounded even younger than she looked. Just how old was the girl?

Sam watched after the couple, not sure how to react. His son was nineteen, an adult under the law. Hopefully the girl was, too. Should he have asked to make sure?

As Josh's van pulled away from the station, Sam's sense of unease grew. He wished Taylor had looked him in the eyes when she'd told him her family knew where she was.

CHAPTER TWO

LEIGH REFERRED TO the MapQuest directions she had taped to the dashboard, next to the cup holder. From the Washington Bridge she was supposed to merge onto I-95.

She did a shoulder-check, then shuddered. A steady stream of cars came up from behind her. Oh, God. Why did all the drivers have to hang on to each other's bumpers? She was never going to be able to make a safe lane change.

But she had to.

She switched on the indicator light, shoulder-checked again, then steered the car to the next lane. Mercifully, the vehicle behind her made room.

Oh, God, she thought again. This traffic was unrelenting. Thank goodness she didn't need to drive very often.

In fact, if the guy at the car rental agency had known just how rarely she did drive, he probably would have thought twice before handing her these keys.

Living in Manhattan, she had no need for a car, which was lucky because she had no interest in them, either. She couldn't even recall the make of this one. It was red and had four doors. When the needle on the gauge fell near empty, it would need to be filled with gasoline. That was the sum total of her automotive knowledge, and she could only pray she wouldn't be called upon to figure out anything else.

She glanced at the MapQuest directions again. In seven-point-three miles she would have to take the Hutchinson Parkway North exit and then almost immediately take another exit to the left.

Usually, Taylor navigated for her. She had a natural sense of direction and was good at reading maps. On top of all that, she had common sense, which was why this whole escapade just didn't compute.

Taylor wasn't the kind of kid to fall in love over the Internet, then run off for a secret meeting. Well, she'd left a note. But a discussion beforehand would have been far more acceptable. Not to mention mature.

If Taylor thought being eighteen and graduating high school was all it took to make you grown up, she had a lot to learn.

"Hey, buddy!" Leigh slowed as a blue car from the right suddenly came into her lane, practically on top of her. Immediately she forgave every rude thing New York taxi drivers had ever said in her presence. Talk about job stress.

Her cell phone rang and she glanced at it, worried. She needed both hands on the wheel. But what if it was Taylor?

She picked it up to check the call display. It was Wenda, the office manager at work. Before she'd left home, Leigh had called and left a message that she wouldn't be able to make it in on Friday. Oh, and by the way, Taylor's graduation party had been canceled.

Wenda was probably panicking right now, but Leigh would have to talk to her later. Right now, the only call worth taking in this traffic was one that might be from her daughter.

Fear tightened her stomach, squeezed her throat. Taylor was okay, she kept telling herself, but what if she wasn't? Only rarely did Leigh regret the fact that she was a single mother. This was one of those times. It would be nice to have a husband to lean on right now. Someone who knew Taylor and who understood that this sort of behavior just wasn't like her.

The police didn't get it. Her call had not been treated with the urgency it deserved. In their eyes Taylor was an adult. The fact that she'd left a note proved she was acting of her own free will.

Just this winter, Leigh had been required to sign the application for Taylor's college admission. Now, if Taylor felt like it, she could enlist in the military and go to war.

As if a few months and a birthday were all it took to make you a grown-up.

The world was a crazy place.

A car on Leigh's tail honked, then pulled out and passed. It seemed to Leigh that the vehicles on both sides of her were driving much faster than she was. She pressed a little harder on the accelerator, gripped the steering wheel a little more tightly.

This was terrifying.

Suddenly, spending a few thousand on a cab fare seemed like a brilliant idea. If only she could take the bus, as Taylor had been smart enough to do. But there was no time. She probably couldn't get to Jefferson before Taylor did, but Leigh was going to get there as fast as possible.

Before PartyMan had a chance to…

No, she couldn't think about that.

According to MapQuest, she had over three hundred miles ahead of her, six hours of driving.

Six hours that her daughter would be at PartyMan's mercy...

"DID YOU CATCH the Red Sox game last night, Uncle Sam?"

"Huh?" Sam flipped a page in the Lands' End catalogue. Lately, his sister had been at him about his wardrobe. It seemed like every item he owned was wearing out. Even the cleaners had told him he needed some new shirts. But what colors? What size? Susan had always bought his clothes for him.

"The Mets trounced them."

He closed the catalogue and looked at Robin, who was grinning at him as he read the sports section of the *Boston Globe*. Robin loved baseball, like just about everyone else in Jefferson—except for Josh and Robin's mom, Kate.

"That rookie pitcher for the Mets is hot. Some say he reminds them of you, in the early years."

"Is that right?" He opened the catalogue again and heard Robin sigh. Poor kid was always trying to engage him in baseball talk. You'd think his mother's aversion to the subject would have turned him off, but it hadn't. Sam's own feelings about the game were ambivalent. Baseball had given him a lot, but it had cost him plenty, too.

"Say, when you were pitching, did you ever—"

The sound of a bell cut Robin short. Outdoor lights illuminated a cherry-colored Ford Fusion as it pulled up to the pumps.

"I'll get this one." Sam tossed the catalogue behind the counter, then moved briskly toward the car. The Fusion's plates told him it was a rental from New York. The driver was an attractive brunette, who must not have noticed this was a full-service station because she was out of the driver's seat before he could ask her what grade of gas she wanted.

She looked to be in her thirties, a petite, pretty woman who radiated tension. He eyed the fancy dress she was wearing. The matching shoes. The slender, yet muscular, calves.

"Can you tell me where Jefferson is?"

He bristled at her tone. A "hello" would have been a nice courtesy. But this woman was clearly in a hurry.

"You're in it." She couldn't have missed the hand-painted sign just a hundred yards up the road.

It wasn't unusual for strangers to have recognized him by now, but this woman's glance was dismissive and short. She was far more interested in the surrounding countryside than the human being in front of her.

"But where are the stores?"

He pointed out the Grocery sign behind him. "Right here. School's around the bend. So's the post office and general store."

As she processed that, he glanced through the window into her car. A black duffel bag was tossed on the back seat. MapQuest directions were taped to the front dash. He smiled at that. On the front passenger seat, along with a cell phone, lay some crumpled tissues and an empty bottle of water.

He gave the woman a closer look. There were smudges of mascara under her eyes. Had she been crying? But she didn't look sad. She looked angry.

"On holiday?" he asked, though she clearly wasn't. She was dressed as if she was on her way to a fancy cocktail party, though that couldn't possibly be the case. Cocktail parties in Jefferson were about as rare as beach parties in the Antarctic.

"No. I'm looking for Oak Valley Road. Do you know where that is?"

She was looking for *his* place? No, he realized suddenly. *Josh's*.

Now he made the connection. This woman had the same delicate build and coloring of the girl Josh had picked up from the bus earlier.

She seemed a little young to be Taylor Hartwell's mother, but Sam would have bet his business that was who she was. The woman was burning off more carbon than any gasoline-sucking combustion engine he'd ever seen.

She was pissed.

He thought of the used tissues in her car and amended his assessment. Also upset.

"Well? Have you heard of it? I hope I didn't write down the address incorrectly."

She looked as if she was about to pull her hair out at that possibility, so he was quick to reassure her. "I've heard of it. Actually, it's my road. My house is there and so is the cabin where my nineteen-year-old son lives."

"Your son. Is he Josh Wallace, by any chance?"

"That's him."

"And you said he's only nineteen?" Her shoulders relaxed a little. "Well, that's one thing I don't have to worry about, at least."

"Pardon?"

"Sorry. I'm just— When I got home from work this afternoon, I found a note from my daughter. She said she'd gone to meet this guy she'd met over the Internet. You can imagine my reaction. She's only eighteen."

Sam swallowed. Yeah, he could imagine her reaction, all right. Good God, what was the matter with Josh? Why hadn't he told him about this? Sam would have advised him to talk to the girl's mother, at least.

"Look, I was about to close up for the night. Why don't you follow me home and I'll introduce you."

He'd have a word with his son at the same time. So much for the hope that letting Josh have his own place would have a maturing effect. Maybe it had been a mistake to let him move into the guest cabin without agreeing on monthly rent. But Josh's event-planning business was still in the start-up phase. Once it was in the black, he'd definitely expect his son to contribute some cash.

"I GUESS WE SHOULD introduce ourselves before we go any further. I'm Sam Wallace."

"Leigh Hartwell."

This man made her feel uneasy. Partly it was his size. He was unusually tall and very broad-shouldered. He was also quite attractive, despite a crooked nose and crowded bicuspids.

Maybe that was the problem. He was *uncomfortably* good-looking. She'd never been able to trust handsome men. They were too used to getting what they wanted from women.

Was that what his son was like, too?

"Right," she said in the brisk, professional tone she used with patients. "So, let's get going." She slipped back behind the wheel, then waited as Sam crossed to the truck parked at the side of the station. A dark-haired teenage boy stepped out from the store and they had a brief conversation. The boy glanced in Leigh's direction, then headed back to the store where he flipped the sign in the door from Open to Closed.

Leigh rubbed the back of her neck as she waited. She was relieved that she'd found the right place, and that her daughter was meeting someone her own age and not an older man who preyed on innocent girls.

Still, there was plenty about the situation she didn't like. Never mind Taylor skipping out on her own graduation party. Why hadn't she told her mother where she was going? That note had been a real slap in the face.

And what kind of kid was this Josh Hartwell? His father seemed respectable enough—not to mention potently attractive—but didn't you have to wonder about someone who would lure a girl hundreds of miles just to meet on spec?

Sam hurried back, keys in hand. He got behind the wheel of a black pickup truck and Leigh hurried to follow him. They passed through the four-way stop, then down a hill and up the next rise.

It was too dark to see much of the surrounding countryside, but Sam drove his truck just under the speed limit, making it easy to follow him. Not that the route was complicated. Oak Valley Road was the second left after the stop sign by the gas station. He could have easily given her directions, rather than going to the effort of escorting her.

Seconds later they pulled into a narrow access road. The track was bumpy and she tightened her grip on the steering wheel as she followed Sam down yet another hill. He stopped beside a white van with "Party Man" painted in black letters, along with a phone number and a Web address.

Leigh felt another release of tension as she realized that Taylor's friend's moniker referred to a business, not a state of mind.

Ahead of them stood a two-story home with white siding and black shutters. It looked like a family home and Leigh half expected a woman to step out the front door with a welcoming wave.

That didn't happen, though. Sam got out of his truck and came around to open her door. He held out a hand for Leigh as she stepped out of the driver's seat.

For a moment they stood close to one another, and Leigh felt a crazy stirring, an attraction she couldn't deny. As a dentist, she was used to being physically close to people she didn't know very well. Some of them were handsome men. But she'd never had this sort of reaction to one of them before. She stepped back, not trusting, not liking, this betrayal of her own body.

"The cabin is just down here." Sam pointed at a worn path to the left of the house. Thanks to a dim porch light, Leigh could see the outline of a small building amid the trees.

She let Sam lead the way, her heels causing her no small problem on the uneven ground. As she stumbled along, fear rose in her again. This was true wilderness out here, with no sign of civilization anywhere, beyond the Wallaces' two homes.

Once on the wooden porch, Sam glanced back at her. He seemed hesitant about knocking.

"Hurry up," she urged him.

"It's awfully quiet in there. I'm a little worried…."

"So am I," she assured him. Her daughter and his son had been alone for hours. Anything could have happened.

She tried the door handle and felt a flood of relief when it turned in her hand. She pushed the door wide and stepped into an open space containing a kitchen, eating nook and sitting area.

No one was there.

Her gaze followed a staircase to the left that led up to a loft.

Sam put a hand on her arm. "The bedroom's up there."

Unbidden came an image of Taylor—bound and gagged and tied to a heavy bed frame. "It's okay, honey. I'm here. I'll be right there."

She tried to break Sam's hold, but it was firm and strong. "Let go of me. What are you doing? Are you crazy?"

"Mom?"

The voice was soft and came from above. Leigh craned her head back. Her daughter stood at the pine railing that ran the length of the loft. She was wrapped in a bedsheet, packaged with the guy next to her like a two-for-one special.

Both had tousled hair, naked shoulders and very flushed cheeks.

There could be no doubt as to what Leigh and Sam had just interrupted.

CHAPTER THREE

"WHAT ARE YOU DOING HERE?" Taylor leaned over the railing, pulling Sam's son with her. Her voice was stronger now and tinged with a defiance that Leigh had never heard before.

"Taylor? What's going on?" It was a stupid question, since the answer was obvious, but Leigh felt completely out of her element. She was relieved, of course, that Taylor wasn't being held against her will, that she hadn't been raped or hurt in any way.

But it was still a shock to find her in bed with this young man. Maybe Leigh should have expected it, but naively, she had not.

"How did you find me?"

"I checked the computer."

"You read my personal messages?"

"Taylor, for heavens' sake! I was worried. I had no idea what you were getting yourself into."

"Didn't you find my note?"

"As if that was any help. God, Taylor. We should have discussed this. You didn't even tell me where you were going."

Taylor groaned. "I wonder why. If only I'd been smart enough to erase my messages."

Leigh put a hand to her neck. Stiffness and neck pain was an occupational hazard. The drive hadn't helped and neither did craning her head this way in order to look at her daughter. "Could you please come down here so we can talk civilly."

"What if I don't want to talk?"

Her daughter's rudeness took Leigh's breath away. As she waited for the moment to pass, the two kids upstairs backed away from the railing, disappearing from sight. From the rustling, Leigh guessed they were putting on their clothes.

Oh, my God. My daughter has just had sex.

The realization hit her hard. Since Taylor had never had a steady boyfriend, this was probably the first time. Why did it have to be with someone she'd met over the Internet? Taylor deserved so much better.

Suddenly Leigh became aware of Sam's presence beside her. He was frowning. "What's your problem?" she asked.

"I'm not sure this is the best time to talk."

"That's my daughter up there. This is the first time she's met your son. And in case you hadn't noticed, they've—"

"I noticed," he said quietly.

"Then how can you even suggest this isn't a good time to talk? What kind of father are you? Those kids—"

"Are adults." He hesitated, and for the first time, uncertainty shaded his dark blue eyes. "You did say Taylor was eighteen, right?"

"Yes. Just out of high school. We were going to have a party...." She glanced down at her dress, so inappropriate for the situation she found herself in right now, but she hadn't wanted to waste a minute changing.

Leigh swayed and immediately felt Sam's hand at her back.

"Let's sit down."

She planted her feet where they were. "I need to talk to my daughter."

"You will. Give them a minute to sort themselves out. Come on, let me get you a drink. You look like you're about to pass out."

Since that was exactly how she felt, she conceded her position and followed him into the kitchen. She sank onto a stool and folded her hands on the butcher-block counter.

Taylor's words were still ringing in her ears. *What are you doing here? What if I don't want to talk about it?*

Her daughter did not speak to her this way. She simply didn't. Clearly, this boy, Sam's son, was to blame.

Sam slid a glass of orange juice in front of her. She glanced up at him.

"Hope that's okay. Only other choice is beer."

That's what he'd picked for himself. She watched as Sam twisted the cap off a bottle of lager, then took a long swallow. She considered asking for a beer, herself, then decided against it and had some of the juice. The beverage slid down easily, and she realized that she was starving. It was almost nine o'clock and she hadn't had anything to eat since lunch.

Sam settled onto the stool next to hers and she was struck by the breadth of his shoulders, the size of his arms. In a flash she saw that she'd been just as foolhardy as her daughter. She'd followed a stranger to a remote location, put herself totally at his mercy.

Logically, it had been a very stupid thing to do. And yet she couldn't summon the energy to feel afraid, or even slightly nervous.

She didn't know Sam Wallace was a decent

person. But she thought that he was. If only she could say the same for his son.

At the sound of steps on the stairs, she turned. Her daughter and PartyMan were dressed and coming to face the music. She studied Taylor's face for signs of contrition and was dismayed to see none.

Before she could say a word, Taylor started.

"I don't see why you had to drive all this way. I'm just visiting Josh for a few days."

"Visiting? It seemed to me you were doing more than *that*."

"*Mom*." Taylor sounded mortified.

"If you wanted to come to New Hampshire, you should have asked."

Josh put his arm around Taylor's shoulders. She smiled at him gratefully, but the smile dropped away when she turned back to her mother.

"You know you wouldn't have let me. Anyway, I don't need your permission anymore."

"Maybe not," Leigh conceded. "But I would have hoped you'd have at least had the consideration to discuss this with me. Or, at the very least, waited an extra day."

"I am sorry about the party, Mom. But you can't blame me for that. I didn't even want one."

Taylor's words stung, mostly because they

were true. Taylor had tried to talk her out of the party, but Leigh had convinced herself that Taylor really did want it. But maybe she'd just been projecting her own wishes on her daughter.

Leigh had never had the chance to celebrate her own high school graduation. She'd been a new mother-to-be by then, taking her remaining credits by correspondence. She'd so much wanted to give her daughter the party she'd never had.

"Look, Mom, I *am* sorry. But there was no other way. You *never* listen to what I say. You don't trust me."

"Maybe for good reason." Leigh waved a hand at Josh. "You've never even met this young man. How could you travel all this way to visit him? He's a *stranger.* I thought you had more sense than that."

"He isn't a stranger. I love him."

Love.

A silence left the word lingering in the air. Josh looked overwhelmed, then he recovered and pulled Taylor closer.

"Love," Leigh repeated. "This is the first time the two of you have met and you're telling me you love one another." Sam hadn't said a word since the kids had come on the scene, but now Leigh turned to him, certain that he had to support her on this point at least.

"Maybe we should leave these kids alone for a bit."

"What?" As far as Leigh was concerned, their discussion had barely started.

"Just give them some space," Sam added, holding out a hand as if he expected her to go with him.

"I'm not leaving without my daughter. Come on, Taylor. We can continue our discussion in the car." The keys were still in her hand. She didn't relish tackling the freeways in the dark, but she supposed she would have to manage.

She started for the door, then stopped when she realized Taylor wasn't following. "Taylor?"

"No."

Josh moved behind her, planting both of his hands on her shoulders. Leigh took a deep breath. "Okay, we don't have to go back to the city. I'll find us a room and after we have a good night's sleep we'll be able to—"

"No, Mom. I won't go with you. Josh invited me for the weekend."

"Taylor, this is crazy. We don't know these men. Come with me and—"

"No, Mom. I'm staying. You want me to, right?" She glanced over her shoulder at Josh.

"Sure." He cleared his throat nervously. "Mrs. Hartwell, we haven't officially met, but—"

"Ms. Hartwell. Not Mrs." Leigh tried not to be swayed by the boy's charming smile. It was a lot like his father's, without the crowded bicuspids. He'd probably had the braces his father had done without.

"Oh. Sorry. Anyway, we haven't met, but I'm Josh Wallace and I do care about your daughter. I didn't trick her into coming to Jefferson. She wants to be here."

"Josh, you're a nice-looking kid and I'm sure you have a lot of friends who think you're great, but what you're doing with my daughter isn't right."

"I have to disagree. There's nothing wrong with what we're doing. This is my place and I'm sorry, but I'm asking you to leave."

"What?" This kid—this boy who had lured her daughter hundreds of miles from home—was kicking her out of his house?

Sam crossed the room. Took her arm.

"Let go of me."

He immediately did so. "You going to exit on your own steam?"

Obviously, she had no choice. She gave her daughter one last look, but Taylor wouldn't meet her eyes. Leigh fought a sudden urge to cry. "If you need me, dial my cell, Taylor. I'll keep it on all night."

It was pitch-dark now and Leigh had to rely on Sam to guide her as she stumbled along the dirt path in her high heels toward their parked vehicles. By the time they reached her rental car, tears were streaming down her face. She averted her head so he wouldn't see.

Taylor had never talked to her that way before.

Was it Josh's influence that was making her do so now? Or was this the result of some parenting mistake Leigh had made along the way? Had she been too protective? Too controlling? Had she somehow forced Taylor into this act of rebellion?

"So," Sam said. "You heading back to New York City now?"

Was he crazy? "I can't just leave her."

"Why not let her stay the weekend, like they planned? I'll drive her to the bus on Monday morning."

How could he say that? "You don't see anything wrong with what they're doing?"

"I admit I'm not one-hundred-percent happy about the situation. But that's not the point."

"It *is* the point. They're just kids. We have to stop this."

"But they're not kids, Leigh." Sam's voice was now gentle.

"I don't care about the technicalities. My daughter demonstrated more good sense when she was ten."

Sam surprised her by smiling. "Love can do that to a person."

There was that word again. In Leigh's opinion people used it far too frequently. Far too easily. "They're young and attracted to one another. All the more reason for us to step in. Their judgment is seriously impaired right now."

"Maybe they're not the only ones." Sam passed her a tissue from his pocket.

Despite the dark, he'd noticed her tears. Leigh blotted them, then sighed. She was so tired. And confused.

"Want to come in for a minute and regroup?" Sam offered.

His house had no lights on, save a dim glow near the front door. In contrast, Sam's son's cottage was ablaze with light. As Leigh watched, first one light, then another, went out. The last one off was in the upstairs loft area.

The bedroom.

Oh, God. Could she really leave Taylor alone like this?

"Leigh? It's okay. Really. I saw the way Josh looked at your daughter. He does care about her. And if you're worried about diseases or pregnancy, don't. I've been very open with my son and Josh knows how to protect her."

Leigh was glad of the dark. Glad that Sam Wallace—new-age dad of the open communications era—couldn't see her blush. "I had those same talks with Taylor." At night. In Taylor's bedroom. In the dark it had been easier to say all the things that needed to be said.

"Good. Then you know we don't need to worry."

As if. Leigh had known, naturally, that one day her daughter would put all that good advice into practice. She'd just hoped that it would be later. And a little more discreetly.

"I need a place to spend the night. Can you recommend someplace nearby? An inn or maybe a bed-and-breakfast?" She'd seen dozens of signs along the highway. There had to be something available in Jefferson, even if it was the smallest town she'd ever been in.

"That's a good idea. It's too late for you to drive all the way back to New York City. Come on inside and we'll phone around."

He cupped her elbow, and she felt it again.

That sizzle of awareness. To counter the effect, she tried to picture him in a dental chair with drool dripping down his chin.

The feeling wouldn't go away.

"Is there a decent place nearby?"

"Several. But it is summer. Tourist season. Finding a vacant room is going to be a long shot."

She let him lead her down a cobblestone walk toward his home. The delicious aroma of stewing meat and vegetables met them at the door.

"Is your wife at home?" Funny she'd been cooking in the dark, though.

"No. I'm a widower."

"I'm so sorry."

"It's been six years," Sam added, his tone a little softer. "That's my dinner in the Crock-Pot you're smelling." He flicked on a series of lights and she saw immediately that the interior of this house was as welcoming as the exterior.

Family pictures on the walls, a hand-crocheted afghan resting on a footstool, candles on the tables.

"Wait there. I'll be right back," he promised as he disappeared down a hallway that ran parallel to a set of stairs leading to the second story.

She took a closer look at the surroundings and saw that the scene wasn't quite as perfect as it first appeared. The potpourri in the crystal bowl near the entrance looked more like dust than dried flowers and pinecones. The curtains in the living room were likewise dusty…and frayed in one corner. The mirror in the entrance was slightly askew.

Six years his wife had been dead?

Other than some superficial cleaning, Leigh was willing to bet the place hadn't been touched since.

"You're sure? Thanks a lot, Kate." Sam's voice grew louder as came back along the hallway. "I'll let you know. You bet."

He disconnected the call, just as he reached her. "Good news. My sister has one room left at her inn. You would have passed it on your way here. It's just a mile from the gas station, on the main highway. Washington Inn…did you notice it?"

"Yes." A cream-colored colonial, with light blue shutters and tons of flowers out front. It had seemed well maintained. She hoped the beds were comfortable. She hadn't realized how tired she was, or how hungry. "Is there a restaurant on the way?"

"Sorry. This is a small town. They sell sandwiches at the general store across from the school, but on weeknights they close at seven."

"You're kidding. There must be someplace where I can find a bite to eat." In New York *nothing* closed at seven. Even her dental clinic stayed open until nine, three days a week. Of course, it was well past nine now.

For a moment Sam didn't answer. He just stared at her. She could guess what he was thinking. Something along the lines of *spoiled city woman has no idea how things are done in the country.*

Well, she didn't care what he thought. She was starving. And she'd had a really, really bad day.

"You're welcome to join me for dinner if you like."

She studied Sam's face. "Are you serious?"

"Why not? I have plenty."

She didn't think she'd endeared herself to him tonight. In fact, she'd been a bit of a pain. "That's very kind of you."

"I'm just being practical. You've been driving for hours, you've admitted you're starving. I've got a Crock-Pot full of stew…more than enough for two."

"It smells divine."

"So you accept?"

He was obviously a very polite man. He even managed to sound like he *wanted* her to stay. "I suppose it wouldn't hurt for us to get to know each other a little better."

And, who knew? Maybe she'd be able to change his mind about how to handle Josh and Taylor. They'd be so much more effective if they were working as a team.

CHAPTER FOUR

"You must have been young when you had Taylor. You don't look old enough to be her mother."

"I *was* young. Only eighteen."

The exact age as her daughter was now. No wonder the sex thing was such an issue for her. Now he'd pressed her hot button again, when all he'd been trying to do was give her a compliment.

Better change the subject. Fast.

"Want some more stew?" She'd already had two helpings, just like him, so he wasn't surprised when she shook her head. He stacked the dirty plates, then pushed them out of the way.

"I was eighteen," Leigh repeated. "And, as you may have guessed, the pregnancy wasn't planned."

He'd hoped to bypass this. Should have known better. "Must have been difficult for you."

"You have no idea."

She was right. He didn't. He and Susan hadn't been much older than her when they'd had Josh, but they'd been in love and excited about starting a family. "What happened to the father?"

"Not in the picture. Never has been. My parents helped me in the beginning. They made it possible for me to go college. I'll always be grateful to them for that."

For that, but not much else, he surmised. "Is Taylor close to her grandparents?"

"Not really. We don't see each other very often. They live in Boston. In the same neighborhood as my sister and her family."

It sounded like there was a lot more than that to the story. But he sure as hell didn't want to hear it. "Want some dessert? I've got ice cream."

"No, thanks." She glanced at her watch. Sighed. "What the heck. I'll run it off tomorrow. What flavors do you have?"

"Maple pecan or chocolate. Are you a runner?" That would explain those great legs.

"Yes. Maple pecan, please. Do you run, too?"

Automatically he sucked in his stomach. He'd managed to pick up an extra pound or two every year since he'd quit ball. "I've been thinking of starting. We have a lot of great trails around here."

He pulled the carton of maple pecan from the

freezer and put some into two bowls. As he did this, Leigh rinsed their plates and stacked them into the dishwasher. Rather than returning to the table for their dessert, they both settled on stools at the counter.

He took his first taste of the ice cream. "Eating this stuff always makes me feel like a kid."

She didn't smile back. "Taylor is not going to make the same mistakes that I did. I won't let her."

Oh, boy.

"Let me tell you a little about my daughter. Taylor graduated from high school this year with a three-point-nine grade average. She's going to work at a coffee shop for the summer, saving her money to go to Cornell in the fall. She's already been accepted."

"Good for her."

Leigh nodded. "The next four years are going to be the best years of her life. I want her to experience everything—living on campus, the social life—as well as her studies."

In other words, everything her mother *hadn't* been able to experience when she'd been that age. "And when the four years are over?"

"An undergraduate degree is just a base these days. Taylor will probably go on to medical school. Or maybe do her masters in psychology."

Did she have an idea how pompous she sounded? Sam couldn't remember meeting anyone who alternately intrigued and annoyed him as much as this woman did.

"What about your son? What are your plans for him?"

She revealed a lot about herself with her questions. "Josh has his own plans. He started his business while he was still in high school. You saw the van out front."

"But what about his *long-term* plans?"

He shrugged.

"A business degree would probably help him if he's serious about running a small company."

"Really? I hadn't thought about that."

Leigh opened her mouth, then closed it when she realized he was being sarcastic. The truth was, Sam *had* wanted Josh to go further with his education. His son knew that the financial resources were available if he ever chose that route. But so far he hadn't.

Leigh pursed her mouth. She did that a lot. It was too bad that a woman with such sweet, kissable lips had such a disagreeable habit.

"I don't care how successful his business is. A college degree would help. It would also provide a safety net for the future. In case his business ever does go sideways."

Sam set down his spoon, even though his bowl was still full. He was no longer in the mood for ice cream. "Look. You may have your ideas about what my son should do with his life. It may surprise you to find out that I have a few of my own, too. But the bottom line is this—it's Josh's life. He's the one who decides if he wants to go to college or not."

"Well, of course he does. But a parent should have some influence in the matter. Though I suppose if he's making all sorts of money at his business, college would be a hard sell."

Sam wasn't going to admit to Leigh that Josh was barely scraping by, that more than once he'd needed to bail out his son so he could cover his payables.

"Sometimes you have to let your kids make a mistake or two."

"There are mistakes, and then there are *mistakes*." She stood and slung her purse back on her shoulder. "I guess we'll have to agree to disagree on that point. Thank you very much for dinner, but I'd better get going now."

"I guess I'll see you tomorrow…?" He followed her down the hallway, then stepped past her to open the front door.

"Yes. I'll be by first thing in the morning to pick up Taylor."

"What if your daughter doesn't want to go home with you?"

Leigh's lips pursed again. "If she insists on staying the whole weekend, I suppose I will, too."

She left then, and he watched her drive away before heading back to the kitchen. Miss Prim and Proper's ice-cream bowl was as spotless as if a kitten had licked it clean.

A YARD LIGHT BURNED bright at the Washington Inn when Leigh drove up ten minutes after leaving Sam's. She parked at the end of a line of six vehicles, grabbed the duffel she'd packed so quickly, then made her way over the stone pathway.

No one was at the front desk when she walked in, but within seconds a woman appeared.

"Hi, I'm Kate Wallace. Welcome to the Washington Inn." Sam's sister had even, pearl-like teeth. She looked around Leigh's age, maybe a few years younger, and was dressed in yoga pants and a matching top. She eyed Leigh's dress and heels with a hint of curiosity, but she didn't offer a comment on the out-of-place outfit.

"Thanks. I'm Leigh Hartwell."

"Yes. So my brother said."

Leigh wondered if Sam had explained the

whole scenario to her. Or told her what a terrible, controlling parent he thought she was. Probably not, because Kate's smile seemed genuinely friendly.

Kate snagged a key from a drawer, then handed her a pamphlet, as well. "I've put you in the turret room. Sorry it's so small, but it was the last room left."

"I'm sure it will be fine." She was desperate to get out of this outfit. Out of these shoes.

On the way, Kate showed her the breakfast room. "Coffee, tea and cookies are available from five o'clock on. Breakfast is served at seven-thirty or eight-thirty. Which would you prefer?"

"Seven-thirty."

Kate smiled. "An early bird."

"No. A runner. I figure if I eat early I'll be able to go for a run around nine. Your brother said you have some nice trails in the area."

"If you aren't afraid of hills, we do. I'm not a runner myself, but many of our guests are. Stop at the desk in the morning and I'll give you a map."

Leigh thanked her, then followed the other woman up a set of creaky, wooden stairs. If she ran for an hour tomorrow, that would make up for skipping her run today and the bowl of ice cream. By the time she showered and drove back to the

Wallace place, it would be around noon, which was perfect since Taylor wasn't a morning person at the best of times.

Which these were not.

On the second story, Kate paused. "To the right is our New England suite. An elderly couple from Canada are staying there. And over here is the washroom you'll be using." She opened the door on the left to reveal a tiny bathroom with a shower stall, sink and commode. "Sorry it's so small, but at least you don't have to share." She passed Leigh the key.

"And my room?"

Kate pointed up and smiled gamely. "You won't need to warm up for your run tomorrow with all these stairs."

The turret room was even tinier than Leigh had expected. And since it really was in a turret, none of the walls were straight. A double bed had been squished into one half of the space. A rocking chair and small footstool sat next to the bank of windows facing the back of the property.

"It's pretty." Leigh fingered a needlepoint cushion on the chair. "How long have you owned this place?"

"I moved here after I was married. The inn has been in my husband's family for decades."

"It must be a lot of work. Do you and your husband run it on your own?"

"My husband passed away six years ago. So it's just me and my son, Robin, now."

"I'm so sorry." Before she could ask what had happened to her husband, Kate was telling her.

"Andrew died in a car accident. He and my sister-in-law were killed instantly."

Oh, no. "Was that Sam's wife?"

"Sam told you about Susan?"

"Only that she'd passed away about six years ago."

"Yes. Andrew was taking Susan shopping in North Conway. She hated to drive in the snow and we'd just had one of those terrible spring storms."

Leigh shook her head in mute sympathy.

"But enough about that." Kate forced a cheerful smile. "I hope you'll be comfortable here. If you start to suffer from cabin fever, feel free to come downstairs for a coffee or to watch television."

"Not tonight, thanks. You don't know how good that bed is looking to me right now."

Kate's smile relaxed. "The bed may be small, but it's really comfortable. I hope you sleep well." She paused in the doorway. "My brother didn't say how many nights you'll be staying?"

"It depends on how long it takes me to talk my daughter into coming home with me. With any luck we'll be gone tomorrow afternoon."

"Sam mentioned something about your daughter. She's a friend of Josh's?"

"Sort of. They met over the Internet." Leigh made a face and Kate looked sympathetic.

"They made a plan to meet the day Taylor finished her last exam. I just found out this afternoon, when I got home from work." She looked down at her dress. "We were going to have a graduation party."

"What a shock that must have been for you."

Leigh blinked away fresh tears. She'd cried most of the way here from New York. As if tears were going to solve anything.

"If it makes you feel any better, my nephew is a sweet guy. He's always been a good kid, never got into any trouble."

"I could say the same for Taylor. Until this."

"Love does strange things to us all."

Sam had said something similar, just a few hours ago. And Leigh had only her own life to look back on to know that it was true. But damn it, she'd hoped Taylor would have known better.

"It'll be okay, Leigh. Get some sleep. And call me if you need anything."

The moment Kate left, Leigh collapsed on the bed and kicked off her shoes. She couldn't think about Taylor right now. It hurt too much. Kate was right. She needed sleep. Things always looked better in the morning, right?

Sam's sister was so nice. Why couldn't Sam be that nice, too?

THE SITUATION DID NOT seem better to Leigh the next morning. It didn't seem better after breakfast, either, and the hour-long run that usually left her feeling clearheaded and optimistic only made her more tense.

She knew she wouldn't feel better until she'd talked to Taylor. Hopefully the implications of her rash actions would have sunk in by now. Wouldn't it be great if she'd already decided she wanted to go home?

Leigh hurried through her shower, then threw on jeans and a T-shirt. In the car she was dismayed to realize the gas tank was almost empty. When she'd stopped yesterday for directions, she'd forgotten to buy any gas.

It was quarter to twelve when she pulled up to Sam's Gas & Groceries. Before she could do much more than unclasp her seat belt, he was by her car.

Why, when practically ninety-nine percent of the gas stations in America were self-serve, did his have to be full-service?

She lowered the window.

"Looking for directions to New York City?"

"Very funny." He was wearing an outfit similar to yesterday's. Dark jeans and a navy T-shirt with the gas station logo embroidered on the front pocket. Inexplicably there was a baseball taking the place of the *O* in the word *Groceries*.

Sam rubbed his chin. "You sleep okay?"

"Just fine."

She felt a subtext in his gaze, a message that came across as clearly as if he'd actually said, *I hope you're feeling more reasonable today.*

"My sister called last night. Said you'd found the place all right."

Had he been worried she wouldn't? That had been considerate of him.

"She said she'd already shown you to your room and that you seemed like a lovely woman."

Leigh was pleased. "I liked your sister, too."

Kate had handled breakfast for ten guests all on her own, without losing her poise and good humor. Clearly, despite the loss of her husband, she was managing just fine. Leigh admired that.

"Kate's one of the best." Sam raised his

eyebrows. "So did you just stop to chat or can I do something for you?"

"Oh, chat, of course, but since I'm here you might as well fill the tank."

"With?"

He was really in a strange mood today. "Gas."

His mouth twitched. "Regular or premium?"

As if she had a clue. She scowled at him. "It's a rental. How should I know?"

"Never mind. I'll give you regular."

Then why had he asked her in the first place? Just to make her feel foolish, no doubt. She watched his reflection in the side mirror as he unscrewed the gas cap, then inserted the nozzle and started the gas pumping. Once everything was set up properly, he grabbed a squeegee and started cleaning her windshield. He was so tall he cleared the bug smears off with three long strokes, leaving a trail of cloudy water with the last one.

"Want me to check the oil?"

Man, cars were a lot of work. "Do we have to?"

"You just picked it up from the rental place yesterday?"

She nodded.

"It's probably okay, then."

He read the total off the gas pump and she handed him her credit card. He returned a minute later. She noted his big, strong hands as he passed her the plastic tray with her card and credit slip. She scratched out her signature, then returned the tray.

"Did you talk to the kids this morning?" she couldn't resist asking.

"They weren't up when I left for work."

She did her best to shut down the mental image he'd just given her. Her daughter in bed with his son, the two of them cuddled up together like…lovers.

She closed her eyes and tried to replace that picture with another—the path she'd jogged along that morning. Rocks and tree roots had made the footing treacherous, but the canopy of birch, oak, maple and pine had more than compensated for that difficulty.

Feeling slightly more calm, she said, "Well, they should be up by now."

"You headed that way?"

"Of course." Where else would she be going?

"Okay. I guess I'll see you there."

"You will?"

"It's noon."

"You go home for lunch?" Why couldn't he just bring a sandwich to work like most of the American workforce?

She didn't want him present when she was talking to Taylor. Didn't want him watching. Interfering.

"I'm not the enemy, Leigh. I'm after the same thing you are. All I want is for my kid to be happy."

Happy, sure. But what about responsible? Considerate? Mature? Leigh didn't say anything, not wanting to start another disagreement.

Leigh took a deep breath, then restarted her car. The pain in her neck had subsided overnight, but she had a feeling she was about to get another.

CHAPTER FIVE

MUSIC BLARED from the open windows of Josh Wallace's cottage. For once the sound of the hip-hop rhythm she usually found so annoying was welcome to Leigh, simply because Taylor liked it, so it was familiar. And precious little had felt familiar to her since she'd started on this unplanned and unwanted voyage of hers.

The path to the cottage was much easier for her to negotiate today in loafers. She hoped that was an omen things were going to go more smoothly with Taylor, too.

Though something told her they wouldn't.

She climbed up the porch stairs and knocked loudly so the kids would hear above the music. It took a few minutes for someone to come to the door. Unfortunately, it wasn't Taylor.

Rather than invite her inside, Josh stepped out onto the landing, closed the door and positioned himself like a guard dog between her and the handle.

He had on jeans, and a tight T-shirt that emphasized his long, lean torso and the breadth of his shoulders. His expression held such a contradictory combination of vulnerability and strength, that for a second Leigh felt a long-forgotten yearning.

The innocence of first love. It really was a wonderful thing in a young person's life.

But then she remembered what love could do to a young woman. She remembered, and she raised her chin high. "I'm here to speak to Taylor."

"I'm sorry, Ms. Hartwell." Josh's tone was respectful, but firm. "She doesn't want to talk to you right now."

"Don't tell me I can't see my own daughter." Why was he doing this? Was Taylor okay? She tried to step past Josh, and when she couldn't, she called out over his shoulder. "Taylor? Are you in there? Are you all right?"

Josh frowned, his composure cracking. "Taylor's fine."

"Why am I not surprised to hear you say that? I'd like to see for myself. Or would you prefer I called the police?"

He shook his head. Gestured her toward the door. "Sorry, Taylor. I tried to tell her—"

"Taylor?" Leigh stepped into a room that

smelled like freshly made toast. Her daughter sat at the kitchen counter with a cup of coffee in her hands. She was wearing a T-shirt on top. Leigh couldn't see what she wore for bottoms.

At least she was safe.

But Leigh wasn't encouraged by the mutinous gleam in her eyes.

"Honey, we need to talk. Could you come outside, please?" Leigh couldn't be here in this house where...everything...had happened. No matter how she tried not to notice details—like her daughter's blouse from yesterday flung on the back of the sofa—she noticed.

Boy, did she notice.

"There's no point in talking, Mom. Josh and I are in love."

Abruptly the music stopped. Josh must have turned the player off. He walked past, headed for the coffeemaker and poured himself a cup. Neither he nor her daughter offered Leigh any.

"Love. Taylor, how can you say that? You barely know one another."

"I knew you wouldn't understand. Josh and I have been e-mailing for a long time. I do know him and he knows me, too, better than anyone, even better than Kerry does. Or you."

Her daughter's words stung, the way they'd

been meant to. Leigh's friends always marveled at how close her relationship with her daughter was. Even during the churning adolescent years, they'd been able to talk, to enjoy time together.

Yet now it seemed that closeness had been a mirage. Secretly, Taylor had been living another life. One that involved the Internet and e-mail and Josh.

Leigh swallowed down the hurt of that and focused on the one thing that really mattered…the well-being of her daughter.

"Fine, Taylor. You don't want to talk, we won't talk. But I'm playing my parent trump card. Get in the car. We're going home."

Taylor's eyes widened, but she didn't move. Slowly she shook her head. Leigh noticed an unexpected glint of silver.

"What's that?" She pointed. "In your ear…did you get another piercing?"

Taylor said nothing. The answer was obvious.

"Josh talked you into that, didn't he?"

Taylor looked at her with disdain. "I've had this for ages. I just didn't wear my stud at home."

Another secret. What else didn't she know about her daughter? "I'm not saying it again, Taylor. Get in the car. Now."

"I'm not going anywhere."

Never in her life had Taylor exhibited such blatant defiance and Leigh didn't know how to react. She couldn't carry her daughter out to the car the way she'd done once when Taylor was two and had a temper tantrum at a shopping mall.

"You may be eighteen, but you're still my daughter and you live under my roof. I buy your groceries and pay for your clothes…."

"Maybe I don't live under your roof anymore. What if I told you I'm spending the rest of the summer with Josh?"

Not just the weekend. The rest of the summer. Leigh's head reeled. "What about your job?"

"I'll find something here."

"You'd better. Because you won't be getting any financial support from me if you choose to move in with this boy."

"Fine by me."

Leigh scrambled to think of something Taylor might still care about. "Your cell phone bill alone comes to more than thirty dollars a month."

Taylor slid off her stool and crossed the room to her backpack. Her legs were bare under the long T-shirt and Leigh's heart ached to see how young and innocent her daughter looked.

This isn't right, she wanted to scream. *You're too young. Way too young.*

Taylor opened the flap, then pulled her cell phone from a mess of clothing and tossed it at Leigh.

Leigh just managed to catch it.

"You can have my bloody cell phone. I don't want it."

Too late, Leigh realized she'd made a mistake. This phone might end up being the only communication link she had with her daughter. But she couldn't back down now so she slid the phone into her purse. "And the credit card?" she asked, her tone as cool as she could manage.

Taylor did some more digging to come up with her wallet. When she found the card her mother had given her for emergency situations, she took it to the kitchen and proceeded to cut it into a dozen tiny pieces.

With each cut, another link between mother and daughter was severed. Suddenly Leigh felt icy cold. What had she done? She'd tried to take a hard-line approach and it had failed.

There was simply nothing she could say or do that would have any impact at all on her daughter.

Taylor seemed to realize that she'd pushed her mother to the edge, because her expression softened. "Go home, Mom. I'll call you once a week. Let you know I'm okay."

How could she be okay? Thanks to Leigh's stubbornness, her daughter was now stranded at an isolated cottage in rural New Hampshire, without any access to emergency funds or her cell phone.

She couldn't leave her here. There was no way. She'd call Wenda. See about a leave of absence. She couldn't go back to the city until Taylor was sitting in the car next to her.

JOSH WAS QUIET after her mother left. Taylor looked at him nervously. "Well, that was fun. Not."

As he bolted the door, Taylor searched the pile of clothes on the sofa for her jeans. She couldn't look Josh in the eyes. She was so mortified. Finding the jeans, she pulled them on and did up the zipper.

"Sorry about that," she mumbled.

Sometimes she hated her mother. She really did. Why did she have to follow her out here and humiliate her this way? And right in front of Josh.

Taylor grabbed her purse and checked to make sure she had her bank card, at least. "I'll catch the afternoon bus," she said. "Do you think you could give me a ride to the gas station?"

"You're leaving? You just told your mother you were staying for the whole summer."

"She made me so mad. I didn't know what I was saying."

Josh took a few steps toward her. "So, where will you go?"

"Maybe my friend Kerry's place…" But she couldn't really see that working. Kerry's mom would feel obliged to call her mother. The truth was, she had no idea where to go.

"You can't go back to New York City. We haven't done anything about your dad yet."

That was true.

"Besides, I don't want you to go." He moved even closer, then reached a hand to her bare arm.

Taylor closed her eyes. She felt so beautiful when Josh touched her. He was gentle and kind. Just like he'd been in his e-mails. Her mother thought you couldn't get to know someone on the Internet. She was wrong.

"This was just supposed to be for the weekend."

"I think we both were a little worried it wouldn't work out. But it has, right?"

She smiled at him. "Yeah. It has." As soon as she'd laid eyes on Josh Wallace she'd known that everything she'd started to feel for him in the months they'd been corresponding had been real.

"So stay."

"Do you really mean that?"

"I do."

If he'd hesitated, it was for just for a nanosecond. It didn't mean he had any second thoughts about his offer. And since she really didn't have a better place to go...

"Thanks, Josh. I guess I will."

LEIGH STUMBLED on her way out of Josh's cottage. And who should be the one to catch her? Sam Wallace, of course.

"What are you doing here?" It shouldn't feel so good to be steadied by a man whose hands felt warm and strong on her shoulders. She stepped away from him as soon as she regained her balance.

"Having my lunch. Just finished my sandwich, as a matter of fact."

She checked the front yard. His truck was there, right between her rental car and Josh's van.

He looked so calm and relaxed, she had a totally uncharacteristic urge to punch him. "You knew all along, didn't you?"

"What did I know?"

The innocent act was too much. "That Taylor intends to stay for the whole summer."

A night had been bad enough. The weekend

had been something Leigh was prepared to negotiate. But the whole summer? Good God, *anything* could happen in two months.

"Actually, I had no idea." A slight frown etched its way between his eyebrows. "Is she planning to stay with Josh?"

"Well, where else do you think she's going to stay? She has no money." Except for her university savings. But Taylor wouldn't touch that. Would she?

The Taylor Leigh thought she knew wouldn't. But the stranger in that cottage? At this point Leigh had to accept that anything was possible.

"Josh doesn't have a lot of money, either."

Leigh raised her eyebrows. "Well, he should have thought of that before he invited my daughter to stay for the summer."

Sam rubbed his chin thoughtfully. "Are you sure that he did?"

"Why are you asking me that? Of course he did. He must have."

"It didn't sound that way when I was talking to them last night."

"You talked to them last night? When?"

"After you left I invited them over for ice cream."

And they'd gone. Leigh couldn't believe it.

The kids had kicked her out of the cottage, but they'd been willing to go to Sam's house for ice cream. How completely unfair.

"What did they say?"

"They gave me the impression that this was just a weekend trip."

"And you believed them."

"Why not? Taylor arrived on the bus with only a backpack. Not a suitcase."

"So the decision to stay for the summer happened later." Was it possible she'd goaded Taylor into it during their argument?

If she'd been more sympathetic, as Sam had suggested, would things be different? Maybe she should have done more listening, less ordering around.

Too late now. Much too late.

Leigh brushed past Sam and headed for her car. Halfway there she heard the music start up at the cottage again. She couldn't tell if it was the same song as before or not. All hip-hop music sounded the same to her.

"Where are you going?"

Sam's question stopped her cold.

Where *was* she going? Was she really going to stay in New Hampshire? Leigh's job was important to her, and not just for financial reasons. The women she worked with were like family. And she felt a responsibility to her clients.

But Taylor was her baby.

"I'm going back to your sister's to see if I can book my room for the rest of the summer." She glanced at the rental that was costing her more than thirty dollars a day. "I guess I'm also in the market for a used car."

"OF COURSE YOU CAN STAY. I'll have a bigger room available on Monday if you like."

Kate was in the kitchen, making blueberry jam. It looked like a lot of work to Leigh. Jars were lined up on a tray to be sterilized in the oven, and a huge pot of blueberries simmered on the stove.

Kate's hands were stained blue, her hair was a mess and her cheeks were pink from the heat.

Why didn't she just *buy* her jam at the store?

"I'm happy with the turret room." It was cozy. Plus, it would be her cheapest option if she did end up staying for the whole summer. Hopefully, though, it wouldn't come to that. Surely, once the first heat of infatuation had cooled, Taylor would see reason.

"It's yours for as long as you want it."

"Thanks, Kate. Good luck with the jam."

The trip to the third story seemed to take a lot

out of Leigh this time. She paused halfway up and finally admitted just how despondent she felt. When she'd left the inn this morning, she'd fully expected to return with Taylor to check out and begin the drive back to New York.

Instead, she'd committed herself to an indefinite stay in New Hampshire. Not to mention an indefinite leave of absence from her job.

Kate had been in the turret room in her absence. The bed had been tidied, the curtains opened and fresh flowers placed in the vase by the window. Leigh settled into the rocking chair, then dialed Wenda's direct number at the clinic.

"Hey, there, it's Leigh. I'm calling from New Hampshire."

"Did you find Taylor? Is she okay?"

"Yes." Leigh rubbed her forehead. She didn't want to admit to anyone what her daughter had done. But Wenda was a friend, as well as a coworker, and she deserved the truth. "She came here to meet this guy she's been corresponding with on the Internet. She claims they're in love."

"Oh, my God. Tell me he isn't ten years older than her."

"He's nineteen."

"Is he a creep?"

"He's nice enough, I guess. Not very ambitious. He has no interest in college, but has a little business and lives in a cottage that his father owns."

Wenda sighed. "It could be worse."

Maybe. But it was pretty bad as it was. "Taylor's quitting her job and spending the summer here."

"Oh, no."

"Exactly. And I can't leave her, so that means I have to stay, too."

"But—"

"I'm not sure when I'll be back. Hopefully before September. I'd like to think it won't take more than a few days, maybe a week, for Taylor to come to her senses, but I can't be sure about that. I'm seeing a whole different side of my daughter. I'm beginning to think the Taylor I thought I knew doesn't even exist."

"You must be so worried. But, Leigh, I'm not sure what we're going to do if you really don't show up until the end of the summer. We can shuffle appointments for a week or two, but…"

"Hire a locum, if necessary. Talk to Judy and Sonia and let me know what they think."

"They'd probably appreciate a call from you, too. Everyone was pretty worried when the party was canceled so abruptly yesterday."

"I will call them. Just not for a few days. I'm a little shell-shocked at the moment."

"Understandable. Okay, I'll take care of things on this end for the next while. And you keep me posted on Taylor. She's a smart girl. Try not to worry too much."

"Thanks, Wenda." Easy for her to say. She had three sons. Leigh disconnected the call.

What to do now?

She wasn't used to having leisure time on a Friday afternoon. In fact, she didn't have much leisure time, period. She and Taylor led busy, almost hectic lives in the city.

She supposed she could read. She hadn't packed a book, but there were magazines in the sitting room. After grabbing her room key, she went back downstairs. It seemed all the other guests at the inn were occupied this afternoon. The old house felt quiet and empty as she sorted through the magazines stacked on the coffee table. Finding a recent edition of *Runner's World,* she settled into one of the couches and started to flip pages.

It felt so decadent to be sitting idly in the middle of a workday. She glanced out the window to the general store across the road. A woman came out with a bag of groceries in one arm and a baby in the other.

Flashback to Taylor at that age. Leigh had been taking classes at university, working a part-time job and living with her disapproving, reluctantly helpful parents. It seemed everywhere she went that year, she had Taylor in one arm and a book in the other. No wonder Taylor had learned to read so young….

She'd been such a clever child and, like Leigh, she'd excelled at school right from the start. Leigh had never had to lecture her about homework or her marks.

She'd never had to lecture her about anything.

Taylor had been the perfect child.

Maybe that was the problem. She'd been too good, and now, in seeking a little balance in her life, she'd gone too far in the opposite direction.

Gone all the way, in fact. With a boy she'd only just met.

Leigh didn't buy the Internet thing. You couldn't really get to know someone via e-mail. So much depended on the look in a man's eyes. The way his hand felt on your shoulder. The smell of him when he was standing right next to you…

Good God. She was thinking about Sam Wallace. Leigh turned another page of her magazine. She couldn't let her thoughts wander this way. Clearly, too much leisure time was a dangerous thing.

But what was she going to do for the next week, possibly more? She couldn't even concentrate on a magazine for half an hour. There had to be something she could do to occupy her time.

She flipped another page and stared at the heading of the article in front of her. *How to Train for a Marathon in Twelve Weeks.*

She'd always wondered if she could run a marathon. The article broke the training into three distinct sections: building up, reaching your peak and tapering off.

She read the first section, which promised if you could run twelve miles—and she could—it was possible to train for a marathon in just three months.

The rest of the article explained how it was done, outlining the training regime on a daily basis. After surreptitiously checking to see if anyone was around, she ripped those pages out of the magazine and folded them into her pocket.

CHAPTER SIX

ON SUNDAY MORNING, Sam sat on the stool behind
the cash register and ran his hands over his knees.
The fabric of his jeans—the last decent pair he
owned—felt soft and thin. He'd checked the
mirror on his last trip to the washroom and
noticed that the collar on his shirt was frayed,
too.

Damn it, he needed new clothes. He couldn't
put it off any longer.

He pulled out the Lands' End catalogue again.
Flipped through the pages. All the men were
slender, clean-cut types. No rough edges, like the
guys he hung around with. Like the guy he *was*.

He imagined that these were the sort of men
that Leigh Hartwell dated in New York City. Guys
with perfect teeth and nice sweaters, who knew the
right color socks to wear with the right color shoes.

The front door opened. A customer walked in.
He didn't look up. "Can I help you?"

No one answered at first. He almost forgot that someone was in the store. Then a shadow fell over the catalogue.

"I like those."

Leigh Hartwell's finger landed on a pair of regular-fit, dark denim jeans. He fought the impulse to toss the catalogue under the counter and pretend he'd only been skimming it out of boredom.

His heart hammering away at his chest, he fought to keep his tone cool and controlled. "Yeah, those look okay. But what size?"

Leigh had been running. She was wearing a cute white hat, sunglasses and a dry-weave T-shirt. Her brown hair was pulled back in a ponytail and her face glowed with sweat. He wondered if she had any idea how sexy she looked.

"You don't know what size jeans you wear?"

"My wife bought all my clothes."

Leigh slipped off her sunglasses and studied him in an analytical fashion. "You haven't bought yourself a new pair of jeans in six years?"

"I like them faded."

"Then maybe you should get these." She pointed to a pair that claimed to be stonewashed.

They did look more comfortable. But she'd

liked the others better. "I don't want something that's going to wear out too quickly. I think I'll go with that first pair. But how do I figure out what size to order?"

"You could check the label on the jeans you're wearing."

Of course. He twisted in a futile effort to see behind himself. "My sister tells me you've booked the turret room indefinitely."

"That's right." She rounded the counter. "I'll take a look if you like. There's usually a patch on the waistband."

He'd only been able to see the top half of her when she'd been behind the counter. Now he checked out the curves of her hips in her tight running shorts. The firm muscles of her thighs and her calves.

He lifted his gaze back to her face. Refocused on their conversation. "Does Taylor know you're staying?"

"I haven't spoken to her since Friday. I thought I'd give her some space for a few days. Turn around," she instructed him, and he complied.

"Finding ways to keep yourself busy?"

"I've done some shopping at the outlet stores in North Conway. I didn't bring much with me from home."

He felt her fingers slip under his belt. "The label is worn out. I can't read the numbers."

He considered making a joke. Asking her to look a little closer. But his mouth had gone dry and he didn't think he could pull it off. He wanted her closer, all right. But to hell with the label.

"Do you have a tape measure?" she asked.

"Sure. In the back. Hang on a minute." Relieved at the opportunity to put a little space between them, he went to the back and searched his tool chest. He returned with a twenty-five-foot measure. "Will this work?"

"A cloth tape would be better, but we'll make do." Leigh pulled out the measure and wrapped it around his waist.

She was close enough for him to smell. Fresh air and good clean sweat. He straightened his posture, squared his shoulders.

"Do you want these jeans to fit?"

Reluctantly, he let out his gut.

"Thirty-two inches."

Was that good or bad? She sounded so matter-of-fact he couldn't tell.

"Now for the inseam." She handed him one end of the tape measure. "Hold this right there." She pointed at his crotch.

He couldn't resist this time. "I'd rather you did."

"I'll bet." She took the other end of the measure and pulled it down to the top of his sneaker. "Thirty-six inches."

His legs were only four inches longer than the circumference of his waist? That couldn't be good. He definitely needed to get into better shape.

She handed him the tape measure.

"So where did you go for your run?"

"Kate gave me a map with some great trails. I just finished a fourteen-mile loop." She fished a bottle of water from the refrigerator section, then opened the fanny pack at her waist and pulled out a five.

He pushed the money back at her. "On the house. Thanks for the tailoring help." He was going to order several pairs of those jeans. "How often do you go running?"

"In the city, three times a week. But since I'm not working right now, I'm going to start running five or six days a week."

"That's pretty intense."

She shrugged.

"Training for a race?"

"We'll see."

She wasn't committing. He wondered why. Was it just her personality? She seemed like one to play her cards close to the chest. That wasn't a trait he particularly liked, and yet, he couldn't say that he didn't like her.

Quite the opposite.

Though her attitude toward his son was annoying, he couldn't really blame her for that. She *was* heavy-handed with her daughter, yet in his books an overprotective parent was better than one who just didn't care.

"How'd you like some company next time?"

She gave him an assessing look. "I'm doing a short run tomorrow, if you want to come along."

"Short would be…?"

"Five miles."

He hadn't run farther than the distance from his car to the front door of his house in over a year. "I think I can handle that."

MONDAY MORNING, an hour before her scheduled run with Sam, Leigh drove up to the Wallace property and parked in front of Josh's cottage. She sat for a moment and stared at the rustic, charming building.

It was still difficult for her to believe that her daughter was in there. Living with a boy. In love.

It had been three days since she'd had her last, devastating argument with Taylor. Three days of hoping that Taylor would give her a call or, better yet, show up at the Washington Inn with her backpack and admit she'd made a big mistake.

But it hadn't happened.

Where had Leigh gone wrong? She must have screwed up somewhere along the line for Taylor to rebel in such dramatic fashion.

Hard to believe that just last Sunday they'd sat down together to watch a movie on TV. They'd ordered Chinese food, made popcorn after. Taylor had seemed happy, normal, *herself.*

And yet there'd been a secret Taylor inside of the girl sitting next to Leigh on the couch. A secret Taylor who was in love with a boy and planning to run away from home in order to be with him.

A newly familiar pain rose up in Leigh and she got out of the car, because she had the feeling that if she didn't move she would die. But once she was outside she didn't know what to do next.

She loved her daughter and wanted her to be happy. This relationship with Josh…odds were against it. They were so young. They didn't really know one another, even though they thought they did. Taylor didn't realize it yet, but she was setting herself up for big-time pain and disappointment.

All the books said that sometimes you had to let your kids make their own mistakes. Was this one of those times? Perhaps her daughter needed more time and she should get back into the car and try again later. Maybe—

The cottage door opened and Taylor stepped outside. She had on a skimpy pair of shorts and a tank top. Bare feet and messy hair that suggested activities Leigh didn't want to think about.

"Mom?"

Leigh restrained herself from opening her arms for a hug. "Are you okay?"

Annoyance flashed in the brown eyes so like her own. "Of course."

Leigh waited for her to ask what she was doing here. Instead Taylor said, "Josh's dad said you booked in to the Washington Inn."

"That's right." Leigh wanted to move closer, but Taylor had a hand on the door frame, poised to bolt.

"What about work?"

"They'll manage without me for a while."

"You don't need to do this, you know."

"I think I do."

"I'm *fine.*"

That's a matter of opinion, Leigh wanted to say, but she didn't.

"I hear you and Sam are going for a run today. That's nice."

Finally, she'd done something of which her daughter approved. "Would you like to join us?" At home, Taylor was occasionally interested in a short run. "We're only going three miles."

"Sam said five."

"Oh, I think he's going to be happy to stop at three."

Taylor grinned. What a beautiful, glorious sight.

"So," Leigh asked, "are you up for it?"

The grin vanished. "I promised Josh I would help him with a birthday party he's planning for the weekend. In fact, I'd better get back in there."

"Wait." Since it was clear she wasn't going to be invited inside, Leigh struggled for something to say that would keep Taylor's attention for another minute or so. "Are you sure you're okay? There's nothing you need? Taylor...you are using protection?"

"God, Mom, I'm not a baby. I've really got to go. I'll talk to you later." She slipped away, slamming the door behind her, and Leigh knew that whatever progress she might have made had been wiped away by that last motherly comment.

"OKAY. I THINK I'm ready for this," Sam said.

He was right where she'd asked him to meet

her, at the start of the Starr-King mountain trail. He had on a pair of track shorts and a T-shirt and though he was clearly out of shape, it was just as clear that he had the body of an athlete.

Leigh focused on the trail map in her hands. "The plan is to run uphill for about twenty minutes, then to turn back. If we have enough stamina we can do it twice."

"Twice, huh?" Sam made a show of stretching his quads. "Shouldn't be a problem."

She recognized male bravado when she saw it, but she didn't challenge him. The mountain would do that for her. She tucked the trail map into her fanny pack, then set the chronometer on her watch. "Ready? Let's go."

She started running along the path, setting a slow pace and keeping an eye on the precarious footing. The path was set with stones that would trip a runner all too easily. All it would take was a twisted ankle to put her racing plans out of reach.

For the first five minutes she felt good. She watched as Sam loped ahead of her a few yards, taking advantage of his longer legs. The climb would take its toll on him soon, she guessed. Anticipating the burn to come, she kept her same slow, steady pace.

Inhaling deeply, she took the time to appreciate the beauty around her. Several of her patients at work were in wheelchairs and she never ran without appreciating the fact that she was healthy and strong. Maybe even strong enough to run a marathon…

She'd always had a secret yearning to attempt one, but the training requirements were daunting for a single mom with a full-time, demanding career. She had friends who'd completed the 26.2-mile race, but the most she'd ever managed was half of that.

Even now, with entire weeks of training time on her hands, she didn't know if she had what it took to complete the whole thing.

She'd committed herself, though. Yesterday afternoon she'd gone on the Internet at the local library, and she'd found a race for late September that sounded perfect. The Adirondack Marathon was only a few hours from New York and it offered beautiful scenery as well as a challenging course. She'd registered online immediately and booked a room at one of the local inns.

Ahead, she could see Sam slowing down. Five minutes later, as she passed him, he admitted, "This is tough." He was breathing so hard he could barely get his words out.

She tried not to grin. "Slow and steady. You can do it."

He grunted and she sympathized with how he felt. Even at a slow pace, hill work was grueling. Her lungs felt as if they were on fire and she no longer had the energy to appreciate the scenery.

Leigh concentrated on the patch of ground immediately in front of her. Dimly, she noted a birdsong and the scolding of a territorial squirrel.

This will get easier with more training, she encouraged herself. Sheer determination kept her moving forward, past the fifteen-minute mark. Sam was falling back, but she kept her original pace.

When he started to gasp, she called a halt. "How about we walk for a minute?"

"I-if you want." He could barely get out the words, but he wasn't going to admit that he needed the rest more than she did.

Men.

She wiped her brow, then twisted around to see how he was doing. Sweat was streaming from his forehead and his face was a deep, dark red.

"You okay?"

"S-sure."

Yeah, right. Not wanting to deal with a heart attack out here in the wilderness, she slowed down further. Maybe this had been too ambitious for Sam's first run. He should have said something. "Want to turn around now?"

"Has it been twenty minutes?"

"Not quite."

"K-keep going."

Finally her watch hit the twenty-minute mark. "Okay, we can head back now." She swiveled to find Sam bent at the waist, his hands resting on his kneecaps.

"Spring training was never this hard."

"What did you say?"

"Nothing." He straightened, wiped more sweat from his forehead. "Okay. I'm good. You?"

Again she had to struggle not to smile. "I'm fine, thanks." She started back down the trail, again setting a nice easy pace and Sam gamely followed.

Going downhill was much easier on the cardiovascular system, but soon Leigh's thighs started to protest. About halfway down, every step was taken with real pain and by the time they reached the bottom, Leigh was grateful to stop.

"You did well," she told Sam. "That was a difficult trail to begin with." She didn't say anything about running it again, and neither did he.

"Want some water?" She offered her bottle and

he had several long swallows, then handed it back. She finished it off. Water never tasted so good as after a run.

Side by side they walked along the highway shoulder toward Sam's gas station, where she'd left her car. Thanks to her level of fitness, it didn't take long for Leigh's heart rate to stabilize. She could tell the run had taken a lot out of Sam, though. He didn't say much until they rounded a bend in the road and the gas station came into sight. She eyed the neon letters perched over the long, squat building.

"Why is there a baseball instead of an *O* in your sign?"

"The designers thought it would be good for business."

"Why?"

He shrugged. "So will you be running tomorrow, or have you earned a day off?"

"Tomorrow I do a recovery run. It'll be longer than today, but no hills."

"Sounds good."

"You want to come?" She was surprised. She thought he'd be scared off after today.

"Sure." He gave her an approving look. "You're in good shape."

"Thanks."

"I had trouble keeping up with you."

No kidding. "You did?"

"A little. But in a couple of weeks I'll be able to give you a run for your money."

"Oh, you think so?" She'd been a serious runner for ten years and he was just starting. She didn't know whether to laugh or be annoyed.

Still, it had been surprisingly nice to have him along. She pulled her car keys from her fanny pack. "Okay, we'll meet here tomorrow at the same time."

"One more thing?"

"Yeah?" She stopped a few yards from the sec-ondhand car she'd purchased off the lot in North Conway and looked back at him.

"I'm having a family dinner tonight. Want to come?"

She stared at him, unable to find words. Her heart rate, which had been quite steady a moment ago, picked up inexplicably.

Sam Wallace was inviting her to dinner? Why?

"Josh and Taylor will be there."

Ah. Of course. He was being polite, inviting her because her daughter would be there. "Thank you, Sam. I'd love to come to dinner."

CHAPTER SEVEN

LEIGH SHOWED UP for dinner a fashionable fifteen minutes late, to find that she was the last to arrive. Sam let her in and accepted the bottle of wine she'd brought.

He looked good in his jeans and T-shirt, both so faded Leigh could tell they'd be soft to the touch. Why hadn't he changed anything in his house or bought any new clothes since his wife died? Was he still in mourning?

The way he looked at her, though, it didn't seem as if he was thinking of his departed wife. She brushed her hands over her skirt and started to slip her feet from her sandals.

"Keep them on. The floor's a little cool in the kitchen. Have you met Kate's son, Robin?" He led her past the living room, where Josh was playing a computer game with the dark-haired boy she'd seen working at the gas station. Taylor was looking a little bored until she spotted her mother, at which point she put a hand on Josh's shoulder and leaned in toward the monitor.

"Good one, Josh," she said, as something exploded in a series of brilliant flashes.

"Hey, Ms. Hartwell." Josh's eyes didn't leave the screen.

"Boys will be boys," Sam said with an apologetic shrug.

In the kitchen his sister was chopping vegetables, U2 was on the sound system and a bottle of wine had been opened and poured. "How's that salad coming?" Sam peered over his sister's shoulder. "Can't you chop any faster?"

"Don't worry about my salad. Concentrate on your steaks. Shouldn't they be done by now?"

"Maybe. If I'd put them on when you told me to."

Kate shot her brother a look.

"Hey. I don't want them overdone." Sam turned down the volume on Bono, then handed Leigh a glass and told her to make herself at home while he put the meat on the outside grill. He grabbed a package from the fridge, then headed to the patio.

"It smells great in here." Leigh perched on a stool feeling very much the outsider, despite Sam's easy hospitality and Kate's welcoming smile. Kate looked so at home in her brother's kitchen, it was clear they did this often.

"You and your brother seem close."

"We always were, but since the accident even more so." Kate brushed cucumber peelings into the trash. "Do you have any siblings?"

"A younger sister. She and her husband and their three kids live in Boston near my parents." Leigh took a sip of wine. "We don't see each other often."

Understatement of the year. She and Taylor made the trip to Boston once a year, at most, and sometimes even that felt too often to Leigh.

"Why? Boston isn't that far from New York."

"We all have busy lives. My parents are both GPs and Pauline and her husband are doctors, too."

She'd sidestepped the real question, as she usually did when the subject of her family came up. Her unplanned pregnancy had changed a lot of things in Leigh's life, including her relationship with her family.

Her mother and father seemed to think they should have a say in every decision she made, no matter how trivial. And her sister was almost as bad. She was always asking how Leigh managed without a husband and offering to set Leigh up with one man or another. She couldn't accept the fact that Leigh was happy being single.

That she *preferred* being single.

About ten minutes later, Sam opened the sliding door. "I hope you're ready, Kate. I'm pulling the steaks off, now."

"Good timing." Kate tossed the vegetables she'd been chopping into a bowl. "Leigh, would you call the kids to the table, please?"

In the living room Leigh found Josh and Robin still playing their game. Taylor was napping next to Josh, but she sprang to her feet at the mention of dinner. She and Josh sat next to each other, holding hands under the table. Sam served the steak, while Kate passed around salad, fresh bread and steamed broccoli.

"This looks *fantastic*," Taylor said.

Kate smiled. "I'm glad you think so. Robin, how about you? Don't you think the broccoli looks fantastic, too?" She handed the bowl back to her son, who reluctantly added a spear to his plate.

Before starting to eat, Sam raised his glass in a toast. "To our visitors, Leigh and Taylor. Welcome to Jefferson and to our home." He glanced around the table, his gaze pausing when it landed on Leigh.

Her breathing turned shallow, her stomach tightened. She wanted to object to Sam's toast, to point out that she was only here because of the very poor judgment of two young adults. But there was a warmth in Sam's expression, and a challenge, too, and both felt personal, as if they had nothing to do with Josh or Taylor.

Was her daughter's boyfriend's father hitting on her?

Surely not.

"So how's work going, Josh?" Kate asked. "Did Lorna call you about the shower for her daughter? It was a last-minute idea, but I told her I thought you could handle it."

"Thanks, Aunt Kate, but I had to turn that one down. Not enough lead time. I promised Taylor I'd take her to the beach next week."

Sam cleared his throat. "Do you think it's wise to turn away work like that when there are bills to pay?"

Josh waved a hand carelessly. "Don't worry. I've got it covered."

"Maybe you've got it covered because I'm not charging you any rent. But that won't go on forever. Remember our deal."

"Living expenses covered for the first year. Yeah, yeah, I remember, Dad. Don't worry."

Robin turned to his uncle, interrupting whatever Sam had intended to say. "Can we turn on the game after dinner, Uncle Sam? The Sox are playing Detroit tonight."

"Hey." Josh tossed a bun at his cousin. "I haven't finished kicking your butt at Super Mario."

Sam didn't seem bothered by the boarding-house manners, but Kate frowned. "Josh. No throwing food at the table, please." She turned to her son, who'd been about to retaliate. Robin took a deliberate bite from the bun in his hand, then smiled. Kate shook her head at his antics. "Maybe we should pick a game the whole family can play. We have that new board game from Christmas."

"Watching baseball is something we could do together," Robin persisted.

"Mom hates televised sports," Taylor said.

"I don't *hate* them. I just rarely have the time for them. Besides, I don't recall you ever turning on the sports network at home."

"I watch baseball all the time at Kerry's."

Did she really?

"At least I recognized Josh's father when I met him. You still don't know who he is, do you?"

Leigh swung her head in Sam's direction. To her surprise he looked a little sheepish. She glanced at

Kate next. Her expression was more difficult to read.

"Sam was a pitcher for the Cincinnati Reds, Mom."

"He was really famous," Robin added. "Want to see his scrapbook?"

"Robin—" Kate held out a hand to stop her son, but she was too late. He'd already skidded out of the dining area in his stocking feet. He returned a moment later with a thick, leather-bound scrapbook. "My aunt Susan made this," he said proudly.

"Maybe after dinner, Josh."

But the proud teenager had already handed her the book and Leigh couldn't resist taking a look. On the very first page a picture of a younger Sam stared up at her. He was wearing a ball uniform and he looked... Wow. There was no other word.

She flipped through a few pages. There were dozens of articles and she skimmed the headlines. *Workhorse Wallace takes Reds to the World Series; Sammy Holds 'Em...blanks Tigers for seven innings.*

"Sammy Wallace." Saying the name quietly to herself, even Leigh recognized it. Damn it. She'd thought he was just the owner of a corner gas station, but he'd been a pro ball player. A *famous* pro ball player.

Kate cleared her throat and Leigh realized that everyone had stopped eating and was watching her. "Sorry." She set the book aside and picked up her fork. She speared a piece of meat, then paused before putting it into her mouth.

She looked at Sam. "Why didn't you tell me?"

Wouldn't most men be proud of a past like that? Before Sam could answer, his son interjected.

"It was a long time ago. Could you pass me another steak, Aunt Kate?"

"Only six years—"

"That's enough baseball for tonight, Robin. Can't you think of something else to talk about?"

Robin sighed, obviously crestfallen. His uncle was clearly his hero. Interesting, though, that Josh didn't seem equally proud of his father. Even Kate appeared rather ambivalent about her brother's fame.

ONCE THE BASEBALL TALK had ended, Sam was able to relax and continue eating his meal. Leigh offered to help clean up the dishes later and he made sure he was the one in the kitchen with her.

"You always say you don't have time to read the paper." He handed Kate the *Boston Globe*. "Here's your chance."

Kate glanced from her brother to Leigh, then gave him a knowing grin. "This is a first. But, hey, I'm not complaining."

She obligingly took the paper to the living room with the kids, leaving him and Leigh blessedly alone. Sam closed the door.

With some women, the more simple their clothing and makeup, the greater their beauty. Leigh was like that. She made a plain red T-shirt and jeans look elegant. As she ran hot water into the sink, he admired the narrowness of her waist, the lean line of her legs in her well-fitted jeans.

"Sorry dinner was a little chaotic."

"Everything was delicious," Leigh responded politely as she added the salad bowl to the sink of soapy water. "I really appreciate your hospitality, Sam, but I have to admit I found the situation a little surreal."

"Josh's manners aren't *that* bad."

"That's not what I meant and you know it. You're welcoming Taylor and me into the family as if you approve of the idea of an eighteen-year-old girl shacking up with a nineteen-year-old boy. Am I really the only one who sees how wrong that is?"

"You're not the only one who sees the potential for trouble," Sam admitted. "We all see that.

But we also see a boy and girl who can't keep their eyes off one another. A boy and a girl who seem to be very happy together."

"Yes, but it's not *real*, Sam. It won't last."

"Maybe it won't. But that's something the kids have to figure out for themselves. We can't do it for them. And, who knows, maybe it will last. Maybe Taylor and Josh will be one of the lucky couples."

Leigh turned to face him. "Like you and Susan?"

He hesitated a moment. "Like me and Susan."

"Do you still miss her?"

Sam hadn't asked himself that question for a while and he had to think about it. "I still think about her, of course. But, no, I wouldn't say I miss her."

He'd gotten used to life on his own, to life as a widower. He hadn't purposefully avoided getting involved with another woman. No one had intrigued him.

Leigh did.

So much so that it kind of ticked him off. He couldn't say she was the perfect choice for him. But neither could he deny the attraction he felt. The attraction that was about to drive him to do something he knew he was going to regret.

"Would you like to see a movie tomorrow night?"

"What?" She froze. "Are you asking me on a date?"

He hated it when women asked that. "What do you think?"

"Nothing personal, Sam, but it's a terrible idea."

Wham. "You sure know how to flatten a guy's ego."

"I told you not to take my comment personally. You have to admit we have several strikes against us—no pun intended."

He groaned. If she only knew how often he heard that one.

"For starters, we live hundreds of miles apart."

"In my defense, I only suggested a movie. Not living together."

Her cheeks pinkened attractively. "Speaking of living together, there's also the issue of my daughter and your son."

"Because they're dating, we can't?"

"They're not just dating. They're living together. We could end up related."

A minute ago, Sam had felt like kissing her. Now, strangulation seemed a more desirable option. "Aren't you jumping the gun, just a little?"

"I'm worried. Any parent would be."

She looked at him accusingly. As if there was something wrong with him that he wasn't worried. "Is there some reason you don't trust your daughter?"

"It's not a question of trust. I want things to be easier for Taylor. This isn't the right time in her life for a serious relationship. She's starting college in September."

"I'm sure a few college students have boy-friends."

"But she and Josh are moving so fast. Who knows where it will end? When I went to college, I had a baby at home and a part-time job. It was not fun, trust me."

On that point, she had his sympathy. He was impressed that she'd stuck with her schooling, made a career for herself. "Taylor told me you're a dentist. How did you manage?"

"My parents helped financially. They paid my tuition and day care for Taylor."

"Maybe you should have tried harder with Taylor's father. He should have been there to help, too."

"I hardly knew Drew…didn't even get his last name."

He was surprised. "That doesn't sound like you."

"You really think you know me that well in less than a week?" She added one last dish to the drying rack, then wiped her hands. "Well, you're right. It wasn't like me. My parents always vetted my boyfriends carefully, but I met Drew when I was on holiday with a friend at her family's cottage."

"A summer romance."

"Basically. At home there were so many rules, so many restrictions. But my friend? She had none, and I just sort of went crazy for those two weeks."

He'd seen it happen. And it was one of the reasons he didn't want to clamp down too hard on Josh. Though he had to admit the boy tried him at times. Like turning down that job Kate had angled for him. That wasn't the way you ran a business. Not if you wanted that business to succeed, anyway.

Leigh glanced at her watch. "It's getting late."

Even though she'd turned him down, he didn't want her to go. "It's only eight. I was thinking we could gather everyone around the table and play gin rummy."

Leigh hesitated, but Kate had just entered the kitchen and overheard his suggestion.

"That's a great idea. Just the excuse I need to pry the boys away from the PlayStation."

Leigh still looked reluctant. "I haven't played cards for a long time…."

But then Taylor came into the kitchen. "Are we playing gin rummy? Kerry and I used to love that game when we were in horse camp. This should be fun."

Leigh said nothing about leaving, then. Silently she took her place at the table. When it came to her daughter, Sam realized, she was going to do whatever it took. As a parent himself, he couldn't fault her for that. In fact, though her methods were different from his own, it was part of what attracted him to her.

CHAPTER EIGHT

AFTER SIX RESTLESS hours, Leigh got out of bed. She did a few stretches, relieved to find she wasn't sore from yesterday's hill work. She didn't think Sam would fare so well, given his lack of training.

Bored in her small room, Leigh went downstairs and searched for signs of life. She found none. Not even hard-working Kate was up this early. In the kitchen, a recipe card for zucchini nut bread lay on the counter, spotted from repeated use. The coffee grinder was filled with fresh beans, ready to go. For a crazy moment, Leigh considered starting breakfast herself...then she shook her head.

What was she thinking? She didn't know the first thing about baking.

She went upstairs and indulged in a long shower, then read for a while. The next time she ventured downstairs, the sun was shining and Kate was humming as she tossed ingredients into an enormous stainless-steel bowl with swift efficiency.

"Good morning. How did you sleep?"

"Fine," Leigh lied. "You?"

"Never long enough. Here." She passed Leigh a mug. "Help yourself to coffee and keep me company for a bit." Robin entered the room then and Kate put a bowl on the counter. "Morning, honey. Here's your oatmeal."

"Thanks, Mom."

The teenager sat at a stool and picked up his spoon. He was a nice-looking kid, Leigh thought as she poured fresh coffee into her mug. He reminded her a little of Drew. He had the same slender build and deep golden tan.

"How long is your shift today?" Kate asked.

"Just until noon."

"Do you think you could mow the lawn when you get home? It's looking shabby."

"Sure. No problem."

Leigh took her coffee and sat on the stool next to him.

"Would you like some oatmeal, too, Leigh?" Kate offered.

"I'll wait until you serve the other guests. I'm still full from dinner last night. Your salad was delicious. Everything was."

"Yeah. Uncle Sam barbecues a mean steak. Did you really not know he used to play pro ball?" Robin's expression was incredulous.

"I really didn't."

"Not everybody loves sports the way you and your uncle do," Kate said.

"But he was on the cover of almost every newspaper when the Reds won the World Series. Then there was the time—"

Kate tapped her watch. "Speaking of time, shouldn't you be getting to work?"

"Oh, yeah." Robin scraped his bowl for the last spoonful, then said goodbye. Kate watched after him, a half smile on her face.

"He's really proud of his uncle."

"He certainly is." Kate sighed.

"That's a good thing, right?"

"Oh, sure."

Leigh sensed there was something she wasn't saying. "But—"

"Robin was young when Sam's career was at its peak. He only remembers the good stuff. The exciting games, the stories in the papers and on the news…"

"There was a downside," Leigh guessed.

"Yes. And it was the family at home that paid it."

"You mean Susan."

"Yes, Susan. But also Josh, who didn't see much of his father for most of his childhood. My husband picked up some of the slack. Andrew took Josh along whenever he and Robin went camping or fishing. He even coached Josh's Little League ball team one year. But Josh didn't take to baseball the way his father had."

Maybe because he resented the sport for occupying so much of his father's time and energy? "Andrew sounds like he was a great father."

"He really was. At times, I know he felt like he was running two households, but he never complained." Kate opened the oven and put two loaf pans filled with batter inside.

How had Kate felt about that, Leigh wondered. Clearly, she loved her brother. But did she resent him just a little, too? Was that why she didn't seem keen to ruminate over his glorious baseball past?

"Sam said you're running again today?"

"Yes. At ten." Leigh helped herself to a refill of coffee. She could sense Kate's interest and felt self-conscious.

"He hasn't dated much since Susan's death."

"Oh. Have you since Andrew's?"

"More than Sam. Not that it's a contest." She laughed. "But it is nice to see him interested in a woman again."

"You mean?"

"You? Don't sound so shocked. It was pretty obvious at dinner last night."

"I'm only in Jefferson until Taylor decides to come home," she reminded her.

"But who knows when that will be. They looked pretty happy last night. You might as well have fun while you're here."

AFTER BREAKFAST, Leigh enjoyed a leisurely read of the morning paper. The trail she'd picked for today was about a ten-minute drive from the inn, and along the way she prepared herself for the possibility that Sam might not show.

In her experience, men often couldn't deal with rejection, no matter how gently you tried to turn them down. She'd lost a number of patients that way, over the years.

But when she arrived at the trailhead, Sam was there, using a tree for balance as he stretched his quads. He grinned and waved and she quickly returned her attention to the road. At least now that she knew he'd once been a professional athlete, his great physique made sense.

As soon as she put the car into Park, Sam stopped stretching and jogged toward her. He was moving a little stiffly this morning, but he still managed to make it to her car in time to open the door for her.

"Good morning," he said.

She returned the greeting, surprised to find out how glad she was to see him. What was the matter with her? Didn't she believe the things she'd told him last night? She should be viewing him as a running partner. The father of her daughter's boyfriend. Nothing else.

"I wondered if you would make it today. Not too sore from yesterday?"

"Not bad."

"Really?"

"Well, maybe I'm a little stiff."

She checked her smile. What was it with men and their macho pride? Anyway, Sam would be grateful she'd picked a nice flat trail for today.

She grabbed her running shoes from the backseat, then took off her shell and tossed it onto the passenger seat. The day was already warm. She wouldn't need it.

She could sense Sam's eyes on her, even when she couldn't see him. As she adjusted the laces on her running shoes, her fingers turned clumsy.

Why was she the one feeling self-conscious here? Shouldn't it be Sam?

But he seemed as relaxed and confident as ever as he made small talk about the weather and the history of the particular trail they were running that day.

Finally, she finished with her shoes. She set the chronometer on her watch. "Ready?"

"You bet."

Though she started slow, Sam kept a few paces behind her on the trail. She tried taking the pace down another notch, but he remained where he was and she grew suspicious.

She stopped running. "Why don't you lead?"

"I prefer the view back here."

She put her hands on her hips and gave him the look that normally sent her dental assistant scurrying. He just grinned.

"Come on, Leigh. Don't act all outraged on me. I think I made it pretty clear last night that I find you attractive."

"I thought I made a few things clear, as well." But if she wasn't interested, then why did she feel so aware of him? Why did his admission that he found her attractive give her so much pleasure?

She started running again and Sam kept abreast of her this time.

"After you left, I thought about what you said. You made some valid points."

"Good."

"Starting a relationship right now probably wouldn't be very smart."

She felt unaccountably disappointed. "I'm glad you agree."

"On the other hand, it's rare for me to meet a woman that I can feel seriously interested in."

Seriously interested? She stumbled over a rock, then corrected her balance. "That's what your sister said. That you don't date much," she clarified.

"The two of you were talking about me?"

"Not really. I mean, it was just a few sentences."

"Don't believe a word she said. I'm not really that wonderful."

She laughed.

"Anyway. Back to the topic at hand. The important thing is that we're choosing to ignore this attraction between us because we're smart. Not because we're scared."

She looked at him skeptically. "If this is some kind of reverse psychology, it isn't going to work."

"Not at all. I'm just saying that I agree with everything you said last night."

"Great. Because I had an idea. Last night at dinner you mentioned that Josh doesn't pay you rent for using your cottage."

"That's true…."

"Then doesn't that give you the authority to decide whether or not he takes in a new roommate? I understand that as a parent you want to give your son space. But as a landlord—"

"Leigh. Stop it. I see where you're headed and I'm not going there." He paused to grab a drink of water and she did the same. Once they were running again he said, "Think back to when you were eighteen. Did you want your mother telling you what to do?"

"My situation was different."

"Yeah, every situation is different, but trust me, all eighteen-year-olds feel the same way. Your daughter is old enough to make her own decisions."

There was truth in what he was saying. But she wouldn't concede the point. She'd seen enough of him and Josh to know that Sam's parenting wasn't perfect, either. "You know, if you weren't financing your son's standard of living, he might be more motivated to improve his education."

"Man, you're stubborn, aren't you?" Sam set his jaw. "Let's just concentrate on the running for a while, okay?"

Several minutes passed before she noticed a signpost ahead, then realized it was the end of the trail. "Want to rest a bit before we turn back?"

"Definitely."

He started stretching and Leigh couldn't help but notice that his muscles were already responding to the running. He must have been in tremendous shape at the height of his career.

"Why didn't you tell me you were a former baseball star?"

Sam lost his balance, then recovered. "I didn't think it was relevant."

"Not even when I asked about the baseball on your sign?"

"I didn't want to put that there. The design firm I hired insisted on it."

"Interesting that you don't have any baseball memorabilia on display in your house."

"Why? So it can collect dust?"

"Is that what your wife used to say?"

"No. Susan was proud of my career. And very supportive. Maybe too supportive."

"You must have been away from home a lot." She pulled out her water bottle, took a couple swallows, while Sam did the same.

He wiped the sheen of moisture from his lips. "Yeah, I was away a lot."

He said it as if it was something he blamed himself for. "You were away playing baseball. Earning a living for your family."

"You've never been on a road trip. There's a lot of time between games, between practices and conditioning sessions. Do you know what I was doing at the exact moment of Susan's death?"

Leigh stuffed the water bottle back into the holder at her waist. They'd ended up in deep territory. Territory she wasn't sure she wanted to venture into any further. But she'd started this. She'd pushed him into talking and so now she'd better be prepared to listen.

"What, Sam?"

"Drinking beer and playing poker with the guys."

She sighed. "That's not so bad. I'm sure Susan—"

"Look. I'm not saying the accident was my fault. But I wasted a lot of time doing things like that when the team was on road trips. Time I could have spent with my wife and my son."

CHAPTER NINE

FOR A MOMENT, Leigh felt a little jealous of Sam's wife. He'd obviously been madly in love with her, even after years of marriage. What would it be like to be in a relationship like that?

Leigh had never come close. The romance that had given her Taylor had been sweet but very short. After Taylor was born there'd been dates but never a big love affair. She wondered what it would be like to be so deeply cherished that six years after your death your spouse still regretted that he hadn't made the most of his time with you.

"You can't be sorry you had a baseball career?" Didn't every boy dream of standing on the pitcher's mound, winning the pennant, the World Series?

"I'm not saying I regret all of it. But if I could go back and change a few things, I would. You know, I wasn't at Josh's birth. He was an October baby, we were in the middle of playoffs."

"You would have missed a playoff game to be at his birth?"

Sam grimaced. "I couldn't have. But there are other choices I would have made differently. That last year of my contract…it wasn't necessary. Financially, we were set. It was just my own ego that made me sign up for the extra year. I didn't want to give up the glory."

"It can't be easy stepping down from a career you love."

"If I hadn't been so selfish, I would have had so much more time with Susan. Who knows, she might still be alive. I should have been the one driving Susan to do her shopping. Not Andrew."

"You can't think that way. The accident wasn't your fault."

"Yeah. I know." He sighed, then checked his watch. "What about it, slave driver? Time to head back?"

"You bet." She started the chronometer running again, then set the pace for the run back to the parking lot. Sam didn't talk much after that and she could tell he was tired. Even without conversation, it was nice to have him by her side. She felt a sense of connection that didn't make sense given how briefly they'd known one another.

Back at their cars, she made notes on their times and congratulated Sam for his efforts.

"You did well," she said. "How do you feel?"

"Better than I did this morning." Sam put one hand on the roof of his truck, used the other to grab his running shoe, then stretched out his quad. The muscle looked rock-solid. She saw him noticing that she was watching him, and felt her skin burn.

"So what's on the schedule for tomorrow?" he asked.

"Maybe you should take a day off and rest."

"Are you afraid I won't be able to keep up?"

"It's a long one tomorrow, Sam. Fifteen miles."

After a pause, he said, "Count me in."

"Are you sure?" She asked the question because she felt she ought to, but she already knew the answer. Sam might wish he had quit his baseball career, but he could no sooner have done that than he could turn down her invitation to run fifteen miles now.

He would be there tomorrow. Whether he'd still be standing at the end of the run was another question completely.

IT WASN'T THAT Taylor didn't love her mom, because she did. And she was also grateful. She knew the sacrifices that had been made on her behalf. Not that her mother complained—she wasn't like that.

But Grandma Hartwell often did. "We come from a long line of medical people, Taylor. Your mother wanted to be an oncologist when she was younger. Did she ever tell you that?"

No. But Grandma Hartwell never lost an opportunity to recount the story, then to explain that her mother had decided to go into dentistry because the hours were regular and the work more conducive to the life of a single mother.

Now, *Taylor* was the one who was going to be a doctor. She would have the whole college experience that her mother had missed out on. Not just the studies, though those were important. But she'd have the extracurricular activities, too. Clubs and sororities and boyfriends.

That was the plan. Had been the plan for as long as she could remember.

And it all made sense to Taylor, it really did. She enjoyed her science classes and she did want a career where she could help people.

Only there were days she felt as if she couldn't breathe. As if there was a map for her to follow and she'd never get a chance to take one step off the path her family had charted for her.

On those days she felt as if there was another girl inside of her. A girl she hardly knew and one her mother definitely didn't.

That was the girl who had started surfing the Net, looking for answers to questions her mother couldn't help her with.

Taylor felt a kiss on the top of her head. Another on her cheek, on her nose, then, oh, so gently, on her lips.

"Josh." She opened her sleepy eyes and smiled.

"You're so pretty when you're sleeping."

He said such wonderful things. Made her feel good and special. Her mother told her she was beautiful all the time. But when Josh said it, it felt true.

She opened her arms to him, then realized he wasn't actually in bed with her, just sitting on the mattress, already dressed.

"Did I sleep in again?"

"It's okay. I would have, too, but I have an appointment at noon."

"Oh, yeah. That historical society anniversary party." The organization was celebrating their one-hundred-and-eightieth anniversary next month and Josh was hoping to coordinate the commemorative banquet and dance. "Should I hurry and get dressed?"

Josh shook his head. "I can handle it. Or maybe I should blow them off and stay with you?"

She didn't dare encourage him to do that. She was coming to realize that it didn't take much to talk Josh out of working.

"Let's go together," she said. "I want to do my share."

"Believe me, if we get this job, there'll be plenty for both of us to do later." He kissed her again. "I'll be back in a few hours. Go back to sleep if you want."

"Good luck, Josh. I hope you get the job." She rolled over, planning to close her eyes for just one more minute. Then she'd get up, do some laundry and clean the place a little.

That was the plan, but she and Josh had been keeping late nights, and the next thing she knew there was someone knocking at the door.

She sat up and checked the time on the clock by the bed.

Oh, crap, it was almost one in the afternoon.

She crawled out of bed, wishing she had a robe, but she hadn't brought many clothes with her and had been sleeping in one of Josh's T-shirts. She wanted to ignore the knocking, but Josh's father had been so nice to them and it might be something important.

The wood floor was warm on her bare feet as she hurried down the stairs. At the front door, she undid the old latch, then peered out into the summer sunshine.

Her mother was on the porch, nicely dressed and made-up.

Double crap. What was her mother doing here?

"Mom?"

"You weren't in bed, were you?"

She wanted to slam the door and run. But if she did that now, she'd pay the price later. Reluctantly, she opened the door wide enough for her to step inside. She stared at the floor, feeling those critical eyes rake over the bed-tousled hair, the rumpled T-shirt, bare legs and feet.

A long moment went by where nothing was said. Finally, Taylor found the courage to look her mother in the eye.

All the disapproval she'd been expecting was there in her mother's expression.

"I didn't see Josh's van in the driveway. Is he out?"

Taylor nodded. "He has a lunch meeting. Would you like some coffee?"

Not waiting for an answer, she headed to the kitchen to put on a pot. While she waited for it to drip through, she poured herself some orange juice, again offering her mother some, and again getting no answer.

"Did you come here to stare at me and give me the silent treatment?"

"Very mature, Taylor." Her mother pulled a packet of papers from her purse. "In case you've forgotten, tomorrow is the first day for registering for classes. You'll want to do it as soon as possible so you have the best chances for your top picks."

Taylor held back the urge to scream. She hadn't forgotten. Last night she'd spent an hour online, reading through the various course descriptions. The effort hadn't really been necessary, since she had all her favorites memorized already.

Why did her mother always treat her like she was a child?

"And don't forget to check out the instructors before you select your classes. I found a site where students have rated their professors on a sliding scale. It looks like there are some real duds, even at Cornell." Her mother pulled out a piece of paper and started reading some of the comments the students had made.

"Okay. I get it, Mom. You can stop now." As Taylor poured herself a coffee, she noticed her hands shaking. "I'll check the professors before I sign up for anything."

"Fine. I'll just leave this on the counter for you. I've also got a list with some of my suggestions. I've done some research and—"

"Mom!" Taylor put her hands over her ears. She couldn't take this anymore. "Who's going to university, anyway? You or me?"

Her mother's lips pursed into a hurt, disapproving line. Taylor had seen that wounded look a lot lately. Why did her mother take everything so personally? As if Taylor's every word and every action was all about her?

"Maybe it should be you going to medical school. It's your dream, after all. Not mine."

"What are you saying, Taylor? You've always wanted—"

"No. You've always told me what I've wanted. The truth is, I have no idea what I really want to do with my life."

"That isn't true. Ever since you were little you've been fascinated by medicine and you excel at all the sciences. It's in your blood. Both your grandparents and great-grandfather were doctors."

Argh! Her mother was so frustrating! "You know me better than I know myself. Is that it?"

"Don't be ridiculous. If you don't want to go to medical school, fine. You can study something else."

"I've had twelve years of studying. Maybe I need a break."

"This doesn't sound like you talking. It's Josh putting these ideas in your head."

"Josh has nothing to do with this conversation. You just want to blame everything on him."

"You and I didn't have these sorts of yelling matches before he came on the scene."

It was true. She and her Mom had gotten along well. Taylor knew some of what she was saying was irrational. Up until now, she had been intrigued by the idea of studying medicine. So maybe her feelings for Josh were a *teeny* bit to blame. But what was wrong with that? Wasn't falling in love supposed to be a good thing?

"You don't want me to be happy. You're jealous of Josh."

It was a cruel thing to say and she regretted it right away. Her mother's face went white, and her body seemed to shrink a few inches.

"You don't mean that, Taylor."

Taylor tossed her coffee into the sink. She owed her mother an apology, but she couldn't get it out.

"Fine. Ignore all my advice. Just don't forget to register for those classes tomorrow."

Taylor wanted to scream. Was college all her

mother cared about? She ran for the door. She had to get out of here.

Her mother followed after her. "Taylor? Where are you going?"

Bloody hell. Would she never leave her alone? "What do you care?"

"This is import—"

"Not to me it isn't."

"Of course it's important to you. This is *your* future we're talking about."

"My future. My future. Do you get it, Mom? Not your future, but mine. And I've already decided I'm not going to Cornell this fall."

She hadn't come to any such decision. The words had just blurted out of her. But seeing her mother's stricken expression, she went for the jugular. "I'm not going to college, period. I'm staying here in Jefferson with Josh."

"Taylor, come back here. You can't issue an ultimatum like that and then just walk away."

Oh, yeah? Just watch me. Taylor turned to run, only to see Josh, frozen on the front porch, his mouth round with shock.

Oh, God. He'd heard everything. What if he didn't want her to stay? They hadn't talked about anything beyond this summer.

"Josh?" She swallowed and waited for him to

tell her that he was sorry but she had to leave. Instead, he walked up to her and put his arm around her shoulders.

Her mom took one look at the two of them, then brushed past and marched, head high, toward her car. Less than a minute later she was gone.

LEIGH WAS WAITING at the trailhead the next day when Sam showed up for their run. Her car wasn't in sight—she must have walked from the inn. It wasn't very far. She had a foot propped on a fallen tree and was tightening the laces on her running shoe. Sam took the opportunity to watch her a bit, before she noticed he was there.

He appreciated the line of her legs, the corded muscles and delicate ankles. Her skin was the kind that tanned the color of a roasted almond. Skin meant for tasting…

But these weren't the kind of thoughts to be having about a woman who'd already warned him she didn't want to get involved. "Leigh?"

She turned her head in his direction. "You're here."

"Don't sound so surprised." He was still sore, but not as bad as he'd been after the hill work. His body was adjusting quite nicely to the new demands he was placing on it.

Leigh switched feet and tightened the other lace. This time instead of looking at her legs, he checked out her expression. She seemed tired and drawn. As he drew closer, he could see how tense she was. "You okay?"

Laces done, she straightened and faced him. "Have you talked to the kids lately?"

Oh, no. "Not since dinner at my house. Why?" There were smudges under Leigh's eyes. He'd guess she hadn't slept much last night.

"Yesterday my daughter informed me that she's changed her mind about college. She's going to stay here with Josh."

"Permanently?"

"I guess."

That was moving mighty fast. Now he understood why Leigh was so tense. He really had to talk to Josh. Having a girlfriend stay for a visit was one thing. A permanent move-in was something else. Leigh was right. There were ramifications to that. Had Josh given them any thought?

"I don't know what she's going to do for money." Leigh sighed. "She's planning to work at Josh's business, but it sounds as if he isn't making enough profit for one person, let alone two."

Sam wanted to argue the point, but in all

honesty he couldn't. Leigh already knew he was letting Josh live in the cabin rent-free.

Maybe he should start charging his son rent, as Leigh had suggested. The idea didn't sit well with him, however. He had so much money, thanks to his ball career, and it made him happy to be able to offer his son a leg up with his new business. As an added benefit, he had to admit he liked having Josh live nearby.

Leigh sank onto the log she'd used for her feet earlier and cradled her head in her arms. "Why is being a parent so difficult? This past week makes toilet training look like a picnic."

He sat beside her. "I know how you feel. It doesn't seem to matter how much you accomplish in life, how educated you become or how much respect you earn in the workplace. We're all on the same playing field when it comes to raising our kids."

"Sam, I'm sorry if I sometimes seem to imply that you don't care about Josh. I know that you do. But honestly, how can you not be concerned that he doesn't want to go to college? In this day and age it's practically a necessity."

"You're right. I would prefer that he went for a degree. But the point in raising children isn't to control them, to make them do what you want or to program their thinking for them."

"You really think that's what I'm doing with Taylor?"

There was trust in her eyes when she looked up at him and Sam felt honored that she would care about his opinion. "Ever heard the expression about giving a person enough rope to hang themselves?"

"Of course. But what if they succeed?"

"In your daughter's case, that would mean that she and Josh ended up married and living here in Jefferson. Would that be such a terrible outcome? Josh is a good guy, from a nice family, if I say so myself."

"But—"

"I know you want the world for your daughter." Once, he'd wanted more than small-town life in New Hampshire for his son, too. But Susan's death had changed that for him. He didn't have the heart to push his son too far from the nest. Not when there was so much lost time between them already.

"Chances are, Taylor does, too," he continued. "But she'll never realize it if you don't give her space to make up her own mind."

"So you're saying that if I stop telling her what

I think she should do, she'll eventually decide to go to college on her own?"

"There's a good chance she will."

"Your approach hasn't worked on your son."

He couldn't say anything to that. Because, damn it anyway, she was right.

"We aren't solving anything here." He stood up, brushed the bark chips from his shorts. "How about we run off some of this steam?"

CHAPTER TEN

THE LAST MILE of the run was tough for Leigh. She could only imagine how difficult it was for Sam. But she had to give him credit. He wasn't giving up. Even though he was sure to pay the price tomorrow.

She breathed in, breathed out, in tune with the rhythm of her stride. The sun was warm on her shoulder blades. Too warm. She could feel the sweat trickling from her forehead, gathering around her neck.

One good thing, though…the extreme physical exertion had managed to clear away the feelings of frustration, disappointment and failure that had been clouding her brain since her argument with Taylor yesterday.

Maybe she had been too controlling with her daughter, but that didn't change the fact that going to university was the right thing for Taylor to do. If she tried Sam's strategy, if she backed off a little and pretended not to care what Taylor decided, maybe her daughter would come to her senses on her own.

She might as well try it. At this point, what more did she have to lose? Never in her wildest nightmares had she imagined that Taylor wouldn't go on to postsecondary education.

Leigh checked the time remaining on her chronometer. "Almost done," she called to Sam, who was trailing right behind her. "Five, four, three, two, one."

"Thank God." Sam stopped running and bent over at his waist. "Am I ever going to hurt in the morning."

"We made good time. At this rate we would—" She stopped, remembering that she hadn't yet told Sam about her race plans. She hadn't told *anyone*.

"What?" Sam brought up the bottom of his T-shirt to wipe his brow. "What would we do?"

"Nothing. I just said we made good time." She had a notebook where she was keeping track of their times and distances, working toward a target of completing the marathon in three hours and thirty minutes. At her age, and given her level of fitness, it was a reasonable goal.

She pulled out her water bottle and drank until it was empty. When she was done she realized Sam was still looking at her, expectantly.

"When are you going to tell me what run you're training for?" he asked.

"What makes you think I'm training for something?"

"Come on, Leigh. You're timing everything we do, measuring distances…" He raised his eyebrows. "It's a marathon, isn't it?"

She wasn't sure why she didn't want to admit it. She shrugged, then stripped off her T-shirt to the running bra underneath. From her gym bag she pulled out a clean shirt. As she turned around she saw Sam watching.

Awareness rippled between them. She swallowed, then broke eye contact, pulling the clean tee quickly over her head.

"Nice abs. Do you do gym work, too?"

"Cross training. Swimming, weights and Pilates." She struggled to get her arms in the sleeves, but her skin was tacky with sweat.

"Let me help." He sorted out her sleeves, then pulled the shirt smoothly over her torso. "Better?"

He still had his hands lightly at her waist. She felt them burning there, on her hot, hot skin.

She could have laughed and stepped back, breaking the spell between them, but she didn't. She saw a lot of men up close in her line of work, but there was something about Sam that went beyond masculine good looks and riveting blue eyes.

It was the way he was looking at *her*.

Her patients never looked at her that way, not even the few men who had dared—despite her brisk, professional deportment—to ask her out after their appointment was over.

Sam was looking at her like he wanted her. And meant to have her.

His hands slid up her arms to rest on her shoulders. "Do you have someone back in New York?"

It took her a moment to realize he was talking about a man. "I don't...I don't—" *Oh, Lord. Spit it out, Leigh.* "I don't date much."

He cupped the back of her head and angled his head. "Why do you get to me? You're right. We live in different worlds."

"Yes."

But did she really get to him? The knowledge made her feel lighter than any woman who'd just run fifteen miles had a right to feel.

"Tell me something."

She raised her eyebrows. She was growing increasingly uncomfortable at his proximity, but still couldn't manage to put even one extra inch between them.

"Do I get to you, too?"

She didn't answer and he didn't seem to expect her to. Instead, he studied her face as if her reply could be found there.

And the next thing she knew, he was kissing her, and she was kissing him back, and it was as if they'd kissed a hundred times before, they were so damn good at it. She loved the way he tasted, the way his mouth fit against hers, the toe-curling way his tongue and hers moved together...

And Leigh was lost, because she never kissed a man this way. It was important not to send the wrong message, important to keep in control and, yet...all she wanted from Sam right now...was more.

Without warning, he pulled back. "Now that wasn't very smart, was it?"

Leigh felt a complete chill pass over her. She wrapped her arms around her waist and fought for equilibrium.

Sam took another step away from her. "I'm sorry."

Instantly she realized that she must have been the one who'd done something wrong. Had she reacted to his kiss too intensely? Shame burned hot in her cheeks. She fussed with the zipper on her gym bag. "I'm sorry, too. That really wasn't like me."

He shot her a quick look and on his face she saw something like anger, but it faded quickly. He brought his shirt up to wipe his face, then gave his head a shake. "I'd better go shower, then get back to work. Do you need a lift?"

"No, thanks."

He'd tied his car key to his shoelaces and as he bent to free it, Leigh focused on the view in the opposite direction. "It sure is pretty countryside." Did her cheery voice sound as fake to him as it did to her?

"Yup," he agreed. Key in hand, he walked briskly to his truck.

As he drove away, she realized he'd said nothing about joining her on her next run. Was this it, then? Had that one kiss blown everything?

Not that there'd been anything to blow... It was just nice to have a running companion. That was all.

"Do you want me to talk to my aunt Kate today?" Josh asked.

He was dressed for meetings in nice jeans and a funky T-shirt. When he'd first sent Taylor a photo over the Internet, she'd been worried that he'd doctored it in some way, but he hadn't. He was just as hot in person. Actually more.

"No. Not yet." Taylor didn't know why she kept putting it off. Josh's aunt Kate was nice—his whole family was nice. Besides, it wasn't as if she was the one who'd done anything wrong.

At the sound of wheels on the gravel lane, Josh headed for the front window.

"It's your mom. I'm out of here. You coming?" Josh grabbed the van keys from the peg by the back door, then waited for her answer. She closed Josh's photo album and put it away. She was sorely tempted to run out with him.

"I'd better stay and hear what she has to say."

"What's the point? She always says the same thing. Who needs all that negativity?"

"You're right. But she's my mom."

He grimaced. Rubbed his temple. "Okay. I'll stay, too."

Josh had a protective streak and she loved it. But she knew it wasn't fair to take advantage of it too much. She didn't want him to be sorry she was living with him. "You don't need to."

Her mother's footsteps sounded on the wooden porch. "If you're going, you'd better hurry…."

He hesitated, then grabbed the door handle just as a knock sounded on the front door. "I won't go far," he said, before disappearing out the back.

Trying not to feel disappointed—she'd *told*

him to go!—Taylor went to face her mother. On a deep breath, she let her in. "Hi, Mom."

Her mother smiled, and it took Taylor by surprise. Her mother hadn't given her many smiles since this whole New Hampshire thing.

"How are you doing, honey?"

"I'm fine." She took a moment to process. "You?"

"Also fine. May I come in?"

The other times she'd been here, her mother hadn't asked. She'd marched inside as if she had every right to do whatever she wanted. "Sure."

Her mother walked to the center of the room, then just stood there.

"Um…want some coffee?"

Her mother nodded.

They settled at the kitchen counter, cradling identical mugs of black coffee.

"So…are you keeping busy?"

That was not the first question she'd expected from her mother. "Very. We have a party for this week and a major wedding to plan for September."

"A wedding?" Her mother's hand shook, spilling coffee to the wooden counter.

"Not *our* wedding, Mom."

"I didn't think that."

Oh, yes, she had. But what puzzled Taylor was why she wouldn't admit it. Her mother never pulled her punches. But maybe she was saving all her ammunition for the university lecture. Any minute now it would start....

So, did you check the Web site like I told you to?

Have you registered for your classes?

You're not seriously thinking of withdrawing your application?

Instead, her mother asked about the party they were planning. Taylor hesitated, considered lying, then decided to just face the music.

"It's a graduation party." She waited for her mother to lambaste her again for the way she'd walked out on her own coming-of-age affair, but again her mother confounded her by saying nothing.

Guilt had her apologizing, anyway. "I really am sorry that you went to all that effort and expense for nothing, Mom."

"Thanks, Taylor, but you were right. I should have asked how you wanted to celebrate your graduation instead of assuming you'd like a party." She reached over to pat Taylor's arm. "It's going to take time for me to get used to treating you like an adult. But I'm working on it."

Oh, my God. Taylor couldn't believe this was actually her mother. "Do you want to hear about the wedding we're planning?"

"Of course." Her mom leaned in closer.

"It's going to be so beautiful. They're getting married outside and the bridesmaids will be dressed in gold. Won't that be stunning against all the autumn foliage?"

"Absolutely."

Taylor went through her and Josh's ideas for decorations, invitations, menus and the wedding cake. "There are so many decisions. I had no idea planning a wedding was this complicated. When we go through the list I feel absolutely panicked, but Josh is so calm, cool and collected about the whole process. He really is good at what he does."

She waited to see what her mother would say about that. Surely she wouldn't be able to resist a gibe about the need for a university education, no matter what you chose to do for a living.

But no.

Her mother said nothing about university, for either Josh or Taylor. They chatted for another twenty minutes, until they'd finished their coffee.

"That was great, Taylor." She washed her cup in the sink, then set it to dry. "Maybe I can take you and Josh out for dinner later in the week?"

"That would be nice…only…this isn't going to be about talking us into going to college, is it?"

"No, it isn't. I've finally realized that you're an adult, capable of making your own decisions about your future."

"Really?" Impossible. This just wasn't the way her mother operated.

"Really." Her mom scooped up her purse, then kissed Taylor on the forehead. "Have a good day, honey. And give me a call once you've checked with Josh on a good evening for our dinner."

"REALLY? DINNER, HUH?" Sam sank into a chair, grateful that his son's call was giving him an excuse to take a break. No sooner had he relaxed, though, than an Explorer with out-of-state plates circled the pumps and stopped by the regular unleaded.

"Robin?"

"I'll get it." The teenager pulled on his Boston Red Sox baseball cap on his way out the door.

"It's like she turned into a different person, Dad. Taylor said it was spooky. She didn't say one word about college or going back to the city, or anything. She was…*nice*."

"That's great, son." So Leigh had decided to take his advice. Sam couldn't help but feel pleased. It was good to know he wasn't enduring all this joint pain and muscle cramping for nothing. Especially since he knew that if he hurt this badly now, it was going to be twice as awful the next morning.

Still, he'd have lots of time to recover. After that kiss, he didn't think she'd be eager to let him run with her anymore. Of course, he could always continue his training on his own. But it wouldn't be nearly as much fun.

"So Taylor and I thought Saturday would be good and we're wondering if you could come with us. Just in case this is a trap and she's planning to corner us, and torture us, until we agree to do whatever she wants."

"Give Taylor's mother the benefit of the doubt. Maybe she just wants a chance to get to know you better."

"She can do that if you're there, too."

"I can't come unless I'm invited, son."

"So ask her to invite you."

"I'll see what I can do."

If only it could be that simple. Sam wondered what his son would say if he knew that his father had kissed his girlfriend's mother.

He still couldn't say what had possessed him. Well, he knew what had possessed him, but why hadn't he shown a little restraint?

Life was a little lonely at times, but it was peaceful. He'd had the love of his life, he really couldn't complain.

A relationship with Leigh would only mess everything up. He'd been thinking about what she'd said that night after the family dinner and he knew she was right. They were so different. Not just where they lived, but their jobs and their history...and yes, even their parenting styles.

"Thanks, Dad. I'll talk to you later, okay?"

"Sure. Bye, Josh." Only after he'd hung up did Sam remember that he'd planned to talk to his son about Taylor and whether it was smart to commit to the relationship so quickly. Then there was that rent business to discuss, too.

Maybe he'd find a better opportunity later in the week.

On the recovery day after her long run, Leigh read a book, chatted to Kate in the kitchen while the other woman baked bread, then spent about an hour on the phone with her office. All the while, she was hoping she would hear from Sam.

But she didn't. So apparently their running dates were history.

The reason she was here in Mount Washington Valley, New Hampshire, Leigh reminded herself, was to safeguard her daughter's future. Not to strike up a romance with a baseball player turned gas station owner.

Still, as she entered his store the next morning, she had to admit that buying a sports drink was only an excuse.

She was hoping to see Sam. Hoping that when he saw her in her running clothes he'd ask to come along.

But Robin was on his own. He was wearing a ball cap and she gave him a second look, bothered by the sense of familiarity she always had around Kate's son. He must resemble one of her patients, but she wished she could remember which one. Leigh plunked a bottle of orange-flavored water on the counter, then dug out enough change to cover the cost.

"Going on a long run?" Robin asked.

"Just a short one, today."

"You practically killed my uncle with the last one. He didn't even come into work yesterday."

"Oh? Is he taking today off, too?"

"Coming in later. I have to go home and help Mom with a few things."

"You work pretty hard."

"I have fun, too. When I finish with the yard today I'm going to a friend's cottage for the rest of the day. We're going to go waterskiing and wakeboarding."

"I remember the summer I learned to water ski. I was scared, but I had a really patient teacher." It had been Drew. He was a natural at all the water sports. She could still remember how thrilled, yet nervous, she'd felt in the water with her ski tips pointed skyward and his hands on her bare waist.

"Want to give it another try? My uncle's boat is in good shape. We could take it out on the weekend."

"Thanks, Robin, but I think my waterskiing days are over." She stopped talking as a pickup truck pulled into the station and parked on the far side of the building.

Her stomach tensed as she watched Sam climb out from the driver's-side door. He was dressed in his running gear and his gaze caught hers the moment he stepped into the building.

"I was wondering where I would find you," he said.

Leigh felt herself blush. "Running can become very addictive."

"Oh? So can other things."

CHAPTER ELEVEN

SAM HADN'T PLANNED on running with Leigh again, but in the end he couldn't stay away. And, if he wasn't mistaken, she'd seemed glad to see him.

So here he was.

They were on the last stretch of an easy six-mile loop. He'd worked through his aches and pains at the beginning and now he felt terrific, as if he could run forever. The relentless training she'd put him through so far was already paying off. A few months of this and he'd feel young and strong again, the way he had when he'd been playing ball.

But it wasn't the physical rewards that had drawn him out this afternoon. It was Leigh. He'd wanted to see her. Simple as that.

And now that he was here he couldn't take his eyes off her. He liked to keep a pace or two behind so he could admire her grace and the athletic lines of her body.

She was in incredible shape.

And he kept imagining how that shape would feel in his arms…

But the daydream wasn't very sensible, because holding her in his arms wasn't going to happen. He wasn't ever going to run his hands down her back or over that firm butt. And he very definitely would never feel those strong, slender legs wrapped around his body—

"That's it. We're done." Leigh slowed to a jog, then to a walk, as she checked the time on her watch. "That was a good pace, but next week I'd like to do it a few minutes faster."

They'd driven to the trail together this time, leaving Leigh's car parked at the gas station. Sam grabbed his water bottle from the front seat and tried to focus on hydration rather than his running partner.

Would she strip off her damp T-shirt again? He waited in anticipation as she pulled something out of her gym bag, but it turned out to be the sports drink she'd bought at the gas station.

She twisted off the top, took a long swallow, then offered him some.

"Water's fine for me."

She tossed the bottle back into her bag, then pulled out a clean shirt. She caught his eye. "You aren't going to kiss me again if I put this on?"

He swallowed. "I suppose I should apologize for that."

"Oh?"

What was going on in that head of hers? Her almond-shaped brown eyes revealed nothing but mild curiosity.

"I should apologize," he repeated, "but it's hard, when I find myself wanting to do the exact same thing again."

Wait. He hadn't planned on saying that.

"Really?" Her eyes were still cool, almost clinically detached, and yet, she took a step toward him. Without breaking eye contact, she reached for the hem of her tank top and in one fluid motion pulled it over her head.

And dropped it to the ground.

"Is that a challenge?"

"I know it isn't smart, but yes, I think it is."

This time he took the extra step and suddenly they were kissing again. He kissed past the orange flavor coating her mouth, finding the essence of the woman he'd started to crave.

For several minutes they were lost and then Leigh pulled back to tell him, "I've decided we can see each other. As long as we set parameters."

His fuzzy brain was slow to process that. "What do you mean by parameters?"

She slipped out of his arms. "Just a few rules. Limits, I guess you could say."

"Such as?"

"We need to remember this is just a short-term thing. A summer romance."

"Is this because you live in New York?"

"Partly. But also because of my history. My relationships with men never last."

He considered that. "Again I ask…why?"

"Sometimes I ask myself that, too. It's a pattern I set with Taylor's father, I guess."

"Maybe it's a pattern you should learn to break." Right now she was acting all cool and detached, but there was warmth in her, passion. He could feel it, pulsing like the blood under her skin.

"Funny you should be the one to say that. You don't date much, either."

Just like that, the tables were turned. "That's true."

He hadn't wanted to date. Couldn't imagine marrying again. Hadn't even looked at another woman with real desire…until Leigh Hartwell drove up to his gas pumps.

"This isn't easy for either of us," he said slowly. "We're not young kids. We're both coming into this with some complicated history."

He still wanted to kiss her. But more than that, he wanted to get to know her. The important stuff. "Tell me more about Taylor's father."

He sat on the trunk of a fallen tree and patted the spot beside him. She hesitated, then pulled on her clean shirt and joined him.

"You were eighteen when you met him," Sam said to help her get started. "You said it was a summer romance and you didn't know his last name. Did you ever try to find out?"

"I didn't. My parents wanted to track him down but I purposely withheld the few details I knew so they wouldn't have any place to start looking."

"Why did you do that?"

"I knew that if they found him it would be ugly. They'd try to force us to get married, or make his family pay a bunch of money and I didn't want that."

"He had a responsibility to you. To your baby." If Sam had a daughter out there, he would want to know about her. No question about it.

"I'm not saying I was thinking straight. In those days, I automatically took the opposite position from my parents. It was a point of principle with me."

He almost laughed. "Sound like anyone you know?"

"Okay, I admit that from the outside it looks like I'm making the same mistakes with Taylor that my parents made with me. But my relationship with my parents was different. I'm not trying to live my life through my daughter. I just want her to have choices."

"She does. And she's making them," he pointed out gently. "As much as we try to prepare them, our kids won't always make the right ones. When you look back, don't you see you made mistakes of your own? And yet, you managed to make a good life for yourself."

"That's true. Certainly the mistakes part is. Maybe the one I regret the most is not telling Drew about our baby."

"Why didn't you?"

"I was hurt that he never called. I'd given him my phone number. I thought he loved me." Leigh shook her head.

"That must have hurt."

"At the time it did."

He would have bought this answer if he hadn't glimpsed the flash of pain in her eyes before she gave it. A part of him was surprised that, even after all these years, she still carried around this wound. But he'd had other hints that Leigh Hartwell was a lot softer than she liked to admit.

"Taylor was my salvation. She was an adorable baby, so happy and fun-loving. As much as I want her to go to Cornell, I'm not looking forward to her moving out of the apartment."

"It was tough at first when Josh moved out. That's why it's important that we parents get on with our lives." Of course, in his case, his son hadn't gone that far.

"I have my work. My running. Good friends. But still." She let out a soft breath. "My home is going to be so quiet."

"Don't make it sound terrible. This could be the start of an exciting new phase of your life."

"Is that what happened for you?"

Again, she had him. His life had been in a holding pattern since Susan's death. And he'd been lonely more nights than he wanted to admit since Josh had moved out. To most of his family and friends he seemed to be doing okay, but Leigh didn't let him get away with anything.

Maybe that was why he found her so hard to resist.

ON SATURDAY MORNING, when Leigh sat down for the late breakfast, Sam was making the rounds with a pot of coffee. He looked out of place in his dark jeans and "Sam's Gas and Groceries" T-shirt. He also looked harried as hell.

"What's going on?" she asked as he filled her mug with a none too steady hand. All the tables were full, and some of the guests were looking a little impatient.

"Kate's sick."

"And so you're cooking breakfast?"

"That's the idea."

"Who handled the early breakfast?"

"Only one sitting today."

Before she could say anything else, he was striding back to the kitchen. Leigh checked the buffet where Kate usually put out cold cereal, milk and jugs of juice. It was empty.

She tossed her napkin on the table, grabbed her coffee, then followed Sam.

Robin was in the kitchen with his uncle. He was sitting by the counter manning the toaster.

"Hi there, Robin. I hear your mom isn't feeling very well."

"I heard her throwing up in the bathroom."

"Oh. Sorry to hear that." She turned to Sam. "So what's on the menu?"

"Scrambled eggs, bacon and toast. I should be able to handle that, don't you think?" Sam grimaced as he whisked a bowl containing at least a dozen cracked eggs. On the stove, bacon was already sizzling and another large pan awaited the eggs.

"How about I put out the juice and cold cereal? Robin, do you know where your mom keeps the cereal?"

Robin pointed at a cupboard. "Cereal's there. Bowls are in the cupboard next to it."

Leigh took the cereal and bowls to the buffet table and assured the guests that their hot breakfasts would be arriving soon. She poured juice, refilled coffee mugs, then started a new pot in the kitchen.

"Thanks, Leigh." Sam gave her a thankful look. "I'm pretty good with a barbecue or a Crock-Pot, but I'm definitely over my head here."

Yet, he'd dropped everything to come and help his sick sister. From what she'd come to know about Sam, she wasn't surprised. "You're doing great."

"How does Kate handle this crowd every morning?" Sam wanted to know as he turned over the crisping bacon. Fat splattered over the stove as he worked. It was going to be a real mess to clean up.

"She makes it look easy," Robin said.

"Which I definitely do not." Sam grabbed a cloth and tried to wipe the grease splatters from his shirt.

Ten minutes later, the eggs, toast and bacon were ready to plate. Leigh carried out the meals, then reported back to the guys that everyone seemed satisfied.

"Thank God that's over." Sam leaned against the stove and wiped the sweat from his brow with the back of his hand.

Leigh surveyed the kitchen. "Not quite…"

Sam followed her gaze. Groaned. "Do we have to clean, too?"

"What do you think?" Leigh started to run a sink of soapy water. A moment later, Sam was rinsing the dishrag and working on the grease splatters. When Robin snuck out to watch TV in the next room, neither one of them said a word.

He'd been a big help on the one day he was supposed to get off from work.

And it was kind of nice to be working in the kitchen together, just the two of them.

"So is Kate going to be okay?"

"She's hoping it's a twenty-four-hour bug. It better be." Sam grimaced. "Lucky for me, my sister is usually very healthy."

And lucky for Kate, her brother was willing to

step in on short notice like this. Sam didn't stop moving until the kitchen was spotless again. As he hung up the dishrag, Leigh felt him brush by her back. She turned and he stopped, and for a moment she hoped he would kiss her.

Instead, he thanked her. "I should get to the gas station. I called in one of my part-time workers, but he has plans for the afternoon."

Once Sam had left, Leigh made a cup of herbal tea and took it to Kate's room. The curtains were closed and the lights were off. At first she thought Kate was asleep. She set the mug on the bedside table, then turned to leave.

"Sam?" Kate rolled over and brushed her hair off her face.

"It's Leigh. Sam's at the gas station and I think Robin just went out to meet some friends."

"Oh, good. How did breakfast go?" Kate sat up.

"Sam took care of it." She hesitated. "Are you feeling any better?"

"Yes. The pills Sam gave me must be kicking in. Would you open the curtains, please?"

"Of course." Leigh pulled them to the side so the morning sun could spill into the room. "It must be wonderful to have a brother like Sam."

Leigh had never had that sort of family support, the kind that didn't come in the form of a bank transfer, or with a load of expectations attached.

"Family sticks together. That's what my father always said."

"I hope my relationship with Taylor turns out to be more like your family's and less like the one I had with my parents."

"You can make it happen. If that's what you really want. It's the parents who set the example."

"I don't mean to sound inept, but how do I do that?" She'd done her best with Taylor, but obviously she'd failed her daughter in some way. How did she correct whatever it was she'd done wrong? She needed to make her daughter *want* to come home. If she'd learned nothing else in the past week, she'd learned that much at least.

"You be there for them. You enjoy them. You try not to judge and especially not to criticize."

"But isn't that a mother's job? To teach and to guide?"

"By example, Leigh. That's the best way. Look, when is the next time you're going to see Taylor?"

"I'm taking her and Josh out to dinner tonight."

"Why don't you make a meal for them here? I won't be using my kitchen, obviously. A house is so much cozier than a restaurant. Make them a nice meal and then just enjoy their company."

"It can't be that simple."

"Actually, it is."

TAYLOR'S FAVORITE MEAL was roast beef with York-shire pudding, so that was what Leigh decided to make. She spent the rest of the morning buying groceries and going through Kate's splattered recipe books. In the afternoon she cooked. She wanted everything done ahead of time so that when the kids arrived she'd be free to do as Kate had suggested...enjoy their company.

At quarter to five, Sam dropped in to check on his sister. Robin showed up moments later. It seemed only courteous to invite them both to dinner, as well. When Taylor and Josh showed up half an hour later she was glad that she had. Having more people meant that there was less of a strain between her and the young couple. The last thing she wanted tonight was a disagreement of any kind between herself and her daughter.

"How's Aunt Kate feeling?" Josh wanted to know.

"Better," Leigh said. "I warmed up some soup for her a while ago and she managed to keep that down. A good night's sleep and hopefully she'll be back to herself tomorrow."

"That's nice of you to help Kate, Mom."

Taylor looked at her speculatively, as if she was seeing something in her mother that she hadn't noticed before.

"I agree," Sam said. "Thank you, Leigh. I couldn't have managed breakfast without you."

Leigh was appalled to find her eyes fill with tears. "I should check the Yorkshires." She didn't know why a simple thing like approval from her daughter and Sam should affect her so much. She opened the oven door. The puddings had risen to golden puffs in the muffin tins she'd used.

"Want me to carve the roast?"

Sam's simple offer brought on more tears, and later, when everyone was sitting at the table, when she had the satisfaction of seeing all the food she'd taken the time to prepare being enjoyed and appreciated and the conversation flowing as naturally as it had the other night at Sam's house, she felt the tears coming on, again.

"Music," she said, needing an excuse to wipe her eyes. "I should put on a CD."

There was a CD player next to the television in the sitting room. She passed through the arched opening and stopped to press her palms to her eyes. She wasn't the sentimental type. What was happening to her?

"Want some help?" Sam had followed her

from the table. He went to the entertainment cabinet and selected some easy-listening jazz.

"Thanks, Sam." He'd seen her tears, she was certain, but she was grateful he said nothing about them. She breathed deeply, pulling herself together. A grouping of photographs on the shelves next to the entertainment unit caught her eye. Robin's school picture from last year was there, as well as one of Kate and Robin from several years ago.

She picked up the final photograph...one of the entire Wallace clan in front of a massive Christmas tree. Right away she noticed the woman standing next to Sam. She was pretty, blond and looked very young. "Susan?"

"God, that photo must be almost ten years old." Sam came up from behind her and put a hand on her shoulder. "Look how young Josh is. And Robin's missing both front teeth."

Leigh's attention drifted to Kate, then to the man standing next to her. There was something about Kate's husband's face that was very familiar.

The resemblance was spooky. Yet undeniable. "What was Kate's husband's name again?"

"Andrew," Sam said.

Oh, my God, was it possible? Were her Drew and Kate's Andrew the same person?

CHAPTER TWELVE

"WHAT'S KEEPING you guys?" Taylor came into the family room just as Leigh was returning the photograph to the shelf where she'd found it. "Should I bring in the pie for dessert?"

Leigh didn't answer her daughter. She was still in shock. "Sam—what was Kate's husband's last name?"

"Dixon. Why?"

He was him, then. She watched as her daughter went to the shelf and picked up the picture.

"Is this what were you looking at?" Taylor asked.

"Yes," Leigh said.

"Oh," she said.

That one word said a lot to Leigh. It didn't register surprise, that was for sure. Leigh studied her daughter's face, but it was suspiciously blank all of a sudden.

Something was going on here.

Had Taylor recognized Drew? But how could she? Leigh didn't have any pictures of Taylor's father. In fact, she still wasn't sure that the boy she'd fallen in love with at eighteen was the same one Kate had married. Surely it defied the laws of probability...

Unless Taylor had found him first.

Was it possible?

"Taylor? Do you recognize the man in that photograph?"

"He's my father, isn't he?"

"What?" Sam had been watching them curiously. Now he looked at them both as if they were nuts. Leigh ignored him. Focused on her daughter.

"As crazy as it sounds, yes, I think so. But... how did you know it was him?"

"It isn't an accident that Josh and I met over the Internet, Mom. I was trying to find my father."

Another bombshell. But maybe she shouldn't be so surprised at this one. At various ages, Taylor had asked questions about her biological father, as any child would. But Leigh had had precious little to offer to satisfy her daughter's curiosity.

"Where would you even start?"

"I found some of your old letters. Ones between you and that girlfriend whose cabin you stayed at that summer."

"You've been talking to Janey?"

"Yes. She remembered you, but she didn't know anything about me. Or about what happened that summer."

"No. We kind of lost touch." Once her parents had found out she was pregnant, they had kept Leigh on a very tight leash. One by one, her friends had stopped calling. Out of embarrassment, Leigh had never confessed to any of them what was really going on in her life.

"Janey told me about the boy you'd been dating. She didn't remember much, but she did know the name of the family where he'd been visiting. I contacted them next and that's how I found out my father's legal name was Andrew Dixon."

Leigh caught Sam's glance and knew what he was thinking. If her daughter could track Drew down so easily eighteen years after the fact, she certainly could have done it, too.

But she'd let hurt and pride stop her. Leigh felt a wave of dizziness. This was all so overwhelming.

"Taylor, why didn't you tell me you were doing this?"

"You never seemed to want to talk about my father. I thought it would upset you."

"That's not fair. If I'd known how important this was to you, I would have helped."

"I'm sorry, Mom. I didn't know. I thought you'd be mad. I was afraid you'd make me stop."

"Wait a minute." Sam put up a hand. "You two are going to have to backtrack a minute here. Are you saying my sister's husband was Taylor's father?" He looked back and forth between them, reading their expressions.

Leigh examined the Wallace family picture again. She didn't blame Sam for sounding skeptical. It was just so fantastical...

"Yes, he was." Despite Leigh's doubts, Taylor sounded confident. "Just ask Josh. He helped me prove it."

Josh. He and Robin were still at the table. So much for the happy family meal she'd worked so hard on. So much for Kate's advice to just *enjoy* each other's company.

"Let's sit down and talk about this." Sam led them back to the dining room. Josh was just returning to his seat.

"Robin went upstairs," he said. "He wanted to check on his mom."

"That's probably just as well." Sam handed the Christmas photo to his son. "Taylor's trying to tell us that your uncle Andrew was her father. Do you know anything about that?"

Josh set his jaw in a look that reminded Leigh

very much of Sam. "It's true. That's why I asked Taylor to come here. I was going to ask Aunt Kate to talk to her about Uncle Andrew. But Taylor and I sort of got sidetracked…"

He held out his hand and Taylor went to him.

Leigh's head started to ache. She still couldn't quite sort this out. "Taylor, I understand that you were looking for information on your father. But can you please explain how Josh became involved?"

"Once I had my father's full name, I did a search on Andrew Dixon and that led me to the Web site for the inn. I contacted Kate without telling her who I was and that's how I found out my father was dead."

Leigh could only imagine her daughter's disappointment at that point. "I'm so sorry."

"I was going to just drop it, but then I got curious about the family. I tried searching Kate's name and that led me to Sam. Then I found the Web site for Josh's party business. He has a blog and I posted, and the rest is history."

Leigh thought of all the PartyMan e-mails in her daughter's computer files. If she'd read more of them, she would have found out about all this sooner.

"At first we talked about my aunt Kate and everything I remembered about Uncle Andrew,"

Josh said. "Then we started talking about other things and realized we had lots in common." Josh and Taylor shared a look so warm and intimate that Leigh had to avert her gaze.

"When were you going to tell me this, Taylor?"

"I don't know."

"Were you *ever* going to tell me?"

"I'm sorry, Mom."

Leigh caught a warning glance from Sam. Did he think she was going to lose her temper? Well, he needn't worry. She was far too hurt right now to be angry.

She'd never kept anything secret from Taylor about her father. Why hadn't she felt she couldn't talk to her about this?

On top of that, it was a shock to find out that her Drew had found happiness with someone as lovely and nice as Kate Wallace. They'd had a son together. Lived a totally different life from the one Leigh had carved out for her daughter and herself in New York City.

The ache in her head was growing more intense. This wasn't fair. She'd tried so hard, worked her butt off, loved her daughter to bits, and yet nothing was turning out right.

"Excuse me, please." She pushed away from the table.

"Mom?"

There was genuine concern in Taylor's voice, but Leigh couldn't deal with her daughter right now. "We'll talk later, Taylor. I need some fresh air. A few minutes alone."

She escaped to the front porch. As the sun set into the White Mountains, she paced the wooden floorboards and tried to come to terms with everything she'd just learned.

There was so much to take in.

More secrecy from her daughter. The realization that the gap between them was even bigger than she'd guessed.

Then the new information about Drew. She'd tried not to think about him over the years, but of course, every now and then she'd wondered. How strange, now, to find herself living in his world. Friends with his wife and his son…

Oh, my lord…Robin. The boy was Taylor's half brother. No wonder he seemed so familiar to her. He was only two years younger than Drew had been that summer they'd fallen in love.

Leigh dropped into one of the deck chairs and sank her head into her hands.

The front door opened behind her. The porch floor squeaked. A hand settled on her shoulder, and she knew immediately whose it was.

"Are you okay?"

Sam's voice was unbelievably tender.

At some point she'd started crying. She must have, because her hands were wet. Everything ached now. Not just her head, but her body and her heart.

Especially her heart.

"Come here."

Somehow Sam pulled her out of the chair and into his arms. Leigh had never realized what a haven a man's embrace could offer. She willed herself to stop crying, even as she rested her cheek against the firmness of Sam's chest.

He stroked her hair, the way she remembered doing for Taylor when she was little and upset. Leigh had never felt anything so sweet.

Once she felt calm enough to speak she said, "I'm sorry I ran out on everybody."

"Don't worry. You've had a shock and Josh and Taylor understand that. We've put away the leftovers and now they're doing the dishes. Taylor said to tell you she loves you."

Leigh almost started crying again at that. But Sam pressed a kiss to her head.

"I think you need a change of scene right now."

She nodded. "Any suggestions?"

"I'd like to take you to my place."

SOMETHING INSIDE of Sam had exploded at the sight of Leigh crying on his sister's porch. Impossible to believe that this was the self-assured, beautiful yet reserved woman who had pulled into his gas station a little over a week ago to ask for directions.

The barrier between Leigh's facade and her inner self had been reduced to rubble. She was exposed at her most vulnerable and he was overwhelmed by the need to comfort her.

At his place he poured her a brandy, which she downed in one swallow.

"More?" she asked.

"I don't think that's a good idea."

The smile she gave him was shaky. "I need a crutch right now."

"Let me be your crutch." He opened his arms, and she came to him, fitting into his embrace snuggly. For all her endurance and strength, he was amazed at how small she was. How delicate.

"I'm sorry for being so weak."

"I would never describe you that way." Her body was all lean muscle, but her strength came from much deeper than that. "The drive that's made you such a good runner has also made it possible for you to raise your daughter on your own and to build a successful career at the same time. You're one strong lady, Leigh Hartwell. Even if you don't feel like it right now."

He ran his fingers over her hair again. He loved the silky feel of it. All he intended, all he wanted, was to make her feel safe. But when her warm breath touched his neck and her arms tightened around him, his body responded.

"Sam?"

Even before he glanced down at her, he knew he was going to kiss her. Knew it was what she was asking him to do.

"Coming here probably wasn't very smart," he said in the instant before their lips touched.

If her kiss was her answer, then it was clear she disagreed.

Though she'd been crying in his arms earlier, her kiss was that of a woman who knew what she wanted. He picked her up—she wasn't very heavy—and carried her to the sofa, settled her in his lap. Not since he'd been a teenager had kissing seemed so wonderfully tantalizing and arousing. He kept his hands under firm restraint, though, fighting the need to touch every inch of her.

He couldn't take advantage of her vulnerability right now. Leigh was unfurling in his arms, open and willing, but he had to resist.

"I should take you back to the inn."

She studied his face. "Is that what you want to do?"

"Not at all."

"Then…" She brushed her nose against his.

He resisted kissing her again. "This is getting pretty intense."

She pressed her mouth to his throat.

"Should I invite you to my bedroom?" He waited, almost hoping she would shoot down the idea.

Instead, she said, "That would be nice."

At those words, hot desire leapt inside of him.

He knew that she was speaking a lie. Sex was not a good idea. It would only complicate the relationship between them.

And yet, he couldn't say no to her. He picked her up for the second time and as he carried her down the hall he considered the mundane details. Did he have protection? And what about clean sheets?

Both were in the spare bedroom, the one that used to be his son's, so Sam took her there.

"You lift me like I'm nothing," Leigh marveled.

"No. I lift you like you're something. Something very special."

She kissed him then like she wanted to possess

him and he let her lead the way, let her set the pace. By focusing on whatever she wanted, whatever she needed, he was able to keep his own body under control, if only just barely.

Whatever happened tonight, he wasn't going to let it be about him.

LEIGH HAD HAD two lovers in her life before Sam. Drew, of course, and then a man she'd met at a dental conference in Boston. She'd left Taylor—ten at the time—with her parents. With the baby-sitter her parents had hired, to be exact. And she and a dentist from St. Louis had had quite the weekend.

Being with Sam was entirely different from both of her previous experiences.

Sam was a lover who knew how to please a woman. More than that, he cared about her, and she felt it in his every touch and every word.

This was something she hadn't expected.

He left her breathless.

And at the end, he held her close to him, with her legs still wrapped tightly around him.

"Don't move," he said.

She didn't answer. She was crying again. Damn it, why now?

"That bad, huh?"

He was trying to make her laugh, and it worked, only the tears kept coming, too. This was something she remembered from when she'd been with Drew, how making love with a man made your heart go all mushy and warm and your emotions rise to the surface.

Sam pulled back a little to look at her and she covered her face with her hands, wiping away the tears, but also shielding herself from him. Gently she disentangled herself from his embrace.

"Leigh? What are you thinking?"

She was thinking of Andrew, but she couldn't tell him that. She was thinking of herself, at eighteen, crying silently at night. Afraid and alone.

There was no alone quite like the alone of being pregnant with no one who loved you by your side.

Her parents had wanted to contact the boy who was responsible for her disgrace, but she had wanted him to contact *her.*

She'd wanted it so desperately, but it had never happened. She'd never heard boo from Drew after their two weeks together.

And in between the months of waiting and the birth of her daughter, she'd grown hard. She'd developed a protective coating without even realizing it.

Every subsequent choice in life she'd made from that point on had been affected by it. Her decision to partner with a group of female dentists. Her decision to join a female running group. She'd purposefully shut men out of her life so that no one could hurt her again.

So what was she doing with Sam right now? Why should this man, right now, be the one to break her pattern?

"I have to get going." She collected her clothing from the floor. What to start with…bra or panties? God, it was awkward getting dressed in front of Sam. She wished he'd avert his gaze, but he didn't.

"What's the rush?"

He raised a good point. She had nowhere to go. No one who needed her. For a woman who had spent the past eighteen years raising a child, that was a scary feeling.

She fastened the clasp on her bra, then looked around for her top. Sam climbed out of bed, not seeming at all self-conscious about his nakedness. He pulled her top out from under his jeans and handed it to her.

"Thanks." She yanked it over her head.

"You still haven't answered my question," he reminded her.

"I don't know what to say. Obviously, I have to go back to the inn. I can't stay here."

"Why?"

"Because...it's awkward, that's why."

"I don't feel awkward." He pulled on his jeans with casual ease, then moved closer and gave her a hug. "Things have changed between us. We should talk about what it means."

The hug felt good. Too good. She could get used to this, and then what? It scared her. "Does it have to mean anything?"

"Are you serious?"

"Okay. It means something. But, Sam, I'm feeling so overwhelmed right now I can't process anything." This much was true. "I haven't thought of Andrew in years. To realize that I've become friends with his widow and his son is mind-boggling."

"I can understand that."

"Then there's Taylor. I've lost my daughter, Sam. I feel like she's turned into a stranger. I thought I knew her so well, but I knew nothing."

"The little girl you loved is still inside of her. You'll always have that. And you can build on it."

She wanted to believe him. She looked around

the room and tried to remember why she was in such a big hurry to leave.

"Don't run away. Leigh, don't you think you've done enough of that in your life?"

CHAPTER THIRTEEN

IN THE END, Sam talked Leigh into staying and watching a movie with him. Then he drove her back to the inn, and walked her to the door. Leigh was surprised at how well she slept after that. In the morning, she dressed quickly, then went to the kitchen to check on Kate.

She found her at the stove, looking like herself again. "You're up."

"You bet. And one-hundred-percent better." Kate added a sprinkling of cheese to the mixture in the large cast-iron pan. "But how about you? Sam told me what happened last night."

That they'd slept together?

"I'm sorry the kids sprang it on you that way," Kate continued. "Though Sam said you had already recognized Andrew from a family photograph."

Kate was talking about Taylor's father. Of course. Where was her head this morning? "I'm still having trouble believing it," she admitted.

"I don't blame you. So am I. I was trying to work out the dates and the best I can figure, I must have started seeing Andrew about two weeks after your love affair."

Only two weeks? Drew certainly hadn't wasted any time. Leigh knew it was ridiculous to feel hurt after all this time, and yet she did.

"I don't think he had any idea you were pregnant."

"No. He wouldn't. I never told him."

"Why?"

"I probably should have. My parents certainly wanted me to. I told myself if he ever phoned I would tell him and if he didn't, I wouldn't."

It was so strange how life twisted and turned on every decision—both big and small—that you made. Drew's decision not to phone. Her decision not to tell him.

"If he were here right now he'd be really upset. Drew had very strong opinions on a father's responsibility."

"Then he should have been a little more careful with his condoms." Leigh shook her head. "Sorry. That came out a little too strong."

"Maybe. But I see your point. I hate to think that I might have been part of the reason Drew never had a chance to be involved in Taylor's life."

If he hadn't met Kate...would he have phoned Leigh? There was no way to know now.

"Poor Taylor. Going to all that work to track down her father, only to find out he'd died."

"Yes. But there must be other family. What about Drew's parents?"

"They've retired to Florida. One day Taylor should meet them. Then there is Robin. He's Taylor's half brother."

"How does he feel about that?"

"We talked last night, but I don't think it's sunk in yet."

"I can relate."

"Yeah. You think you know a person and then you find out something like this."

Kate touched her finger. Leigh realized it was the place where she would have worn her wedding ring.

"Andrew never told me about you," she said, staring out the window. "You'd think he would have, wouldn't you?"

AFTER BREAKFAST, Leigh was surprised to get a call from her daughter. It was the first time since she'd arrived in Jefferson that Taylor had made any effort to get in touch with her.

"Can we talk, Mom? I'm really sorry about last night."

They met at the general store. Leigh bought them both ice-cream cones and they sat on a wrought-iron bench outside, overlooking the Presidential Range.

"It's cool how they've named the mountains after former presidents, isn't it? Josh says he and his dad have climbed all the big ones: Washington, Adams, Jefferson and Monroe. There's more," Taylor added. "I can't remember them all."

Leigh closed her eyes. She wanted to pretend that they were sitting in Central Park, the way they had so many Sunday afternoons. Enjoying a treat and nice conversation. She and Taylor had never had trouble talking to one another.

Taylor had always enjoyed hearing about Leigh's day at the dental office. The work was more interesting than most people assumed. You met some real characters in the dental chair, that was for sure.

And she enjoyed hearing about Taylor's friends, about her teachers, about the subjects she was studying at school.

But had they ever talked about the stuff that really mattered?

"Honey, did I ever tell you why I named you Taylor?"

"You said it was because James Taylor was one of your favorite musicians."

"Yes. But there's a bit more to the story than that."

"Oh?"

Leigh could feel Taylor's interest like a palpable presence in the air between them. She so rarely offered her daughter this sort of information. The really personal kind.

"The summer that your dad and I were together...we spent all our time at the lake." Leigh smiled, remembering. "Your dad was very athletic. He was always trying to impress me with his diving."

She had no pictures, but she could remember how Drew had looked poised on the edge of the swimming dock. His slender, masculine body and golden-brown, smooth skin. He'd always called her name, just before he dove, as if he was afraid she might turn away at just the wrong moment.

Look at me! Leigh! And then he would jump.

A teenage boy, trying to impress his girl. And she *had* been impressed.

"And every night, after dark, we'd sneak away from the group of teenagers who hung out at the wharf. We'd tuck ourselves into one of the empty ski boats that belonged to one of the neighbors, and we'd watch the stars and talk."

"Just talk, Mom?"

Leigh smiled.

They'd made out, too, of course. Often for hours. And always stopping just at the brink.

And then, the last night, they hadn't stopped. She hadn't said no. They were listening to a tape they'd found in the boat. It was a compilation recording from the eighties and Leigh had never forgotten the name of the song playing at that all too crucial moment.

"Were you in love with him?" Taylor asked.

"Oh, yes." Would Taylor be grossed out if she told her the specifics? "You were conceived in the back of a Malibu ski boat…."

"I was?"

Leigh nodded. "With James Taylor singing 'Country Road' in the background."

"Really? You're kidding. That's so romantic."

Leigh almost smiled, then her mothering instincts kicked in. "Actually, it was very irresponsible. We should have—"

"Mom?"

"Yes?"

"Can we skip the lecture this time?"

"But—"

"I'm not a kid anymore. I'm a woman."

"I know," Leigh said quietly. But she wished she didn't. She didn't want to face the fact that her daughter was in love and engaged in an active sex life.

Where had the years gone?

And would she ever regain the bond with this grown-up Taylor that she'd had with her own sweet baby girl?

ON MONDAY MORNING, Leigh used her calling card to check in with Wenda at the office.

"How is Taylor?"

Leigh wasn't sure how to answer that. She didn't want to admit that Taylor had decided against college. She was still hoping to change her mind on that one.

Then there was the whole topic of Taylor's father…again, that seemed too big for a telephone conversation.

"She's okay."

"Still living with that guy?"

"Josh Wallace. Yes, she's still with him."

"And you're still not very happy about that," Wenda surmised.

"Not at all. But I'm trying to pretend I am. It's the only way I can keep Taylor talking to me." Sam's advice seemed to be working, and Leigh intended to do her best to keep following it. As she'd seen yesterday when she and Taylor went out for ice cream, any time she shifted into mother mode, her daughter retreated.

And there was already so much distance between them, so she couldn't let that happen.

"How are *you* doing?"

"Besides being worried sick about Taylor?" Leigh ran her fingers through her hair. As soon as she was finished this call she planned to put her hair into a ponytail and meet Sam for a run. "I've been training, and that's keeping me sane. Doing a lot of hill work and some long distances."

"Training for anything in particular?"

Although she'd registered for the Adirondack Marathon, Leigh said nothing about it. Her goal of running a full marathon still seemed too big to put into words. "Just keeping busy."

"Well, you won't have that problem for much longer. When can we expect you back here?"

"That's why I was calling. Wenda, do you think the office could manage until the beginning of September?"

Long silence greeted her question.

"I'm sorry. I don't want to cause extra work for Judy and Sonia. Have you looked into hiring a locum?"

"I've made a few inquiries. But we were hoping it wouldn't be necessary. Leigh, your patients don't want to see another dentist. They want *you*. Most of them are refusing to book their appointments until you get back. I don't have to tell you what a scheduling nightmare this is becoming. And it's hurting the bottom line, too."

Leigh thought fast. There was no way she was comfortable leaving Taylor alone in New Hampshire. At the same time, she couldn't ignore the demands of her practice. Judy, Sonia and Wenda, as well as her patients, deserved better.

"Tell you what. I'll drive back to New York for a few days next week. Book me in for Tuesday, Wednesday and Thursday and make them long days. Try to get the most urgent cases in, if possible."

"That will help," Wenda admitted, grudgingly. "And I'll talk to Judy and Sonia again, about hiring a locum. We should be able to take care of the regular checkups and simple fillings, at least."

"Thanks, Wenda." Leigh disconnected the call feeling vaguely dissatisfied. When it came to her work, she was a perfectionist. But her partners were just going to have to cope. Taylor's future was more important than anything else right now.

Kate walked by then, carrying a tray of fresh cookies for the sitting room. "How are things in New York?"

Leigh had told her she was planning to phone the office. "Okay, I guess. But I'm afraid my patients—and my partners—are feeling a little neglected."

She followed Kate into the other room, watched as the other woman set the tray on the sideboard.

"Do you like being a dentist?"

"I do. It's very rewarding work."

"Aren't most of your patients afraid of you? I know I dread going to the dentist."

"I hope my patients don't feel that way. I'm sure most of them don't. We've become friends over the years." She had some patients who she had to book for double time slots because they always chatted so much.

Kate glanced at Leigh's shorts and tank top. "So what are you doing now? Going for a run?"

"Shortly. Why?"

"I was just going through a box of old photos in the kitchen. I've invited Taylor over and I thought you might be interested, as well."

"Photos of Andrew?"

Kate nodded. "I called Andrew's doctor this morning, too. We talked about releasing his medical history to Taylor. It will require a bit of paperwork, but I've already set that in motion."

She'd never thought about Taylor's father's medical history. "Is there anything we should be worried about?"

"Not at all. Andrew was a healthy man, and so were his parents."

"Thank you for thinking of that."

"Actually, I didn't. Taylor asked me and I was happy to call Andrew's physician on her behalf."

Leigh wondered if Taylor had been worried that there might be genetic medical problems in her family history. She'd never talked about any such concerns with Leigh, but Leigh could no longer be surprised about that.

It seemed Taylor had kept a lot of her questions and concerns to herself over the years.

"Yes, I'd love to see the pictures," she told Kate.

Taylor arrived at the inn about ten minutes later and the three women spent over an hour looking through Kate's albums. Kate even had photos of Andrew as a child, including the baby book his mother had made for him.

Everyone was always remarking on the similarities between Taylor and her mother, so Leigh was surprised to see a striking resemblance between Andrew's baby photos and Taylor's.

Her daughter seemed tickled by the similarities. "I think we have the same nose." She pointed at her father's high school graduation picture. "Don't you?"

"Absolutely." Leigh could tell it was important to Taylor to come up with something, no matter how small, to link her directly with her biological father.

"Pick out your favorites," Kate told Taylor, "and I'll have copies made for you."

"I'll put together my own album of my father." Taylor sounded delighted. "Thanks so much, Kate."

Sam showed up just as Taylor was finishing with her selection. Leigh wished she could treat his unexpected appearance as nothing special, but since they'd made love she felt as if her body had been tuned to his. Just having him near heightened her senses…as well as her pulse.

She did her best to give nothing away, though.

After saying hello to his sister and her daughter, he raised his eyebrows in her direction. "I thought we were going for a run?"

"I distracted her," Kate said quickly.

"We've been looking at pictures of my dad," Taylor added.

Sam glanced at the box, then at Leigh. "Want to put off the run until tomorrow?"

Though it was subtle, there was something different in the way he looked at her now. A trace of intimacy that Leigh hoped the others didn't notice.

"No. I'm still up for a short one. I just need to go back to my room for a second."

She said goodbye to her daughter and thanked Kate again for retrieving Andrew's medical history and photographs for Taylor. She ran up to her room and quickly tied her hair back, then grabbed her cap and sunscreen. Sam was waiting in his truck.

"We might as well ride in one vehicle."

"Sure."

Sam drove to a trail that was becoming one of Leigh's favorites and they ran for a good forty-five minutes. As they were cooling down, Leigh waited for her heart rate to settle back to normal, but it wouldn't.

She knew Sam was to blame.

He was waiting for her to strip off her damp tank top, she knew he was. For some reason the sight of her bare midriff seemed to turn him on. And the prospect of that happening was both exciting and scary.

"Leigh?"

She was so breathless she could hardly respond. "Yes?"

"Tell me what you're training for."

"Huh?" This wasn't what she'd been expecting.

"Whatever it is, I want to run it with you. Let me know so I can register."

She expelled a long breath, not sure if she was disappointed or relieved. "You were right when you guessed the other day. I've registered for the Adirondack Marathon in late September."

He nodded. "I thought so."

"You serious about signing up?" It was a big goal for someone who'd only started training a few weeks ago. Yet his former conditioning was holding him in good stead.

"I'd like to try." He grabbed a towel from the truck and scrubbed at his hair and his face. "Want to come to my place for a drink?"

Wham. Just when she hadn't been expecting it, he'd put it out there. "A drink?"

He caught and held her gaze, then reached for her hand.

"Just a drink?" she asked again.

He pulled her closer. "What do you think?"

CHAPTER FOURTEEN

"SO HOW DID it feel looking at all of those photographs of Andrew?" Sam asked.

"Strange. And yet nice. Those pictures filled in a lot of blank spaces for me. And for Taylor."

Leigh sat at the counter, engulfed in Sam's terry bathrobe. They were finally having the drink he'd promised her. Her hair was wet and her cheeks were flushed and he thought she looked absolutely beautiful.

In bed she was unexpectedly passionate, and also disarmingly shy. The combination was endearing to him and so at odds with his first impression of her.

"Does it upset you that he married someone else?"

"I'm glad Drew found happiness with Kate and that they had a son together. The timing was a little…quick. But I keep reminding myself that he didn't know I was pregnant."

The way Sam saw it, if Andrew had slept with her, he'd owed her a phone call, at least. So the fact that Andrew never had a chance to be involved in Taylor's life was partly his own damn fault.

"Looking at those old pictures also made me realize what a huge adjustment it must have been for your family when Drew and Susan died."

"Yes." Sam's gaze went to the cross-stitch picture above the kitchen table. Susan had worked for years on that. Finally finished it and had it framed about six months before the accident.

"Andrew was a great guy," he continued. "Always willing to give Susan and Josh a hand when I was out on the road."

"Kate said as much."

"My sister paid a price, too." Sam wove his fingers through his hair. So many people had sacrificed so he could have his *big* career. Sometimes he really wondered if it had been worth it.

"Have you talked to Taylor yet?" he asked.

"We had a nice chat today. You know, she used to ask me questions about her father all the time when she was little. As she grew older, she stopped asking, but I guess she never stopped wondering. I'm glad she's finally getting the answers she needed."

Leigh finished her juice, then headed to the family room. She fingered the afghan on the sofa—another one of Susan's craft projects—then circled back to the kitchen.

"I should get going." Her voice was brisk and falsely cheerful.

He didn't want her to go. "You could always spend the night."

She smiled, but offered no other answer. As she made her way to the bathroom, he knew she was going to get dressed. A moment later, he heard the water go on.

They'd showered together after their run, then had spent about an hour in the guest bed again. He wanted to take her back there, now, but obviously she wasn't ready to spend the entire night with him, yet.

He wandered into his own room to get dressed so that he'd be ready to drive her home. His and Susan's wedding picture on the bureau was the first thing to catch his eyes. There were more family pictures on the wall, plus another cross-stitch. Even the duvet cover was something Susan had made.

About a month after the accident, Kate had come over to the house to help him pack up Susan's clothing. They'd boxed the better items for charity and tossed out all the rest, including Susan's personal effects—tubes of lipstick, jars of creams and containers of eye shadow.

After that first, major purge, it hadn't occurred to him to do any other house cleaning.

But now he saw that Susan—her presence and her touch—was all over his house.

He picked up the wedding photo. Ran a finger gently over Susan's radiant face. Susan. In the months and years after her death, his memories of her had faded, but he could still imagine her voice calling him and Josh to dinner. In any situation he knew what she would say, what she would do.

He'd known her so well.

And knew he'd never forget, but since he'd met Leigh, he thought of her much less frequently. Even now, looking at her picture, he could feel the distance.

It was scary, in a way. Part of him wanted to cling to her, to focus on the past, to *make* himself remember as vividly as he once had.

No, Sam. Don't do that. It's time. I want you to let me go.

It was what Susan would say if she was here. She'd always had a generous heart. Her ability to give was something that inspired him still.

RUNNING HAD BEEN an important part of Leigh's life for years. Now it became her number one focus.

Unless she counted Sam.

But she didn't count Sam. She didn't think about Sam or what their time together meant to her. What was the point? Come September, when Taylor was safely enrolled at Cornell, she'd be back in New York and all this would end.

Summer romances were her specialty. Best to enjoy what they had without worrying about the future.

She and Sam ran together almost every day now. Leigh charted their distances and times, accumulating all the statistics in a notebook. Every day after checking her work e-mail, she researched training for marathons on the Internet.

The next day, she shared any new information with Sam, but mostly he was content to follow her lead when it came to their training regimen. And often in bed, too, he seemed happy to let her call the shots. She was surprised to find out she could be adventurous in bed. She could be bold.

On Sunday, after a long run and a much longer lovemaking session, she was in Sam's arms, staring over his shoulder and out the window of the spare bedroom. Several times she'd considered asking him why he always took her here, rather than to his own room. But she already knew the answer had something to do with Susan.

Sam's wife had been dead for six years, and still he honored her memory.

She had to respect that, even though sometimes she resented being in the runner-up category. When that happened, though, she cautioned herself not to develop too many expectations. Susan had been a forever kind of love. Leigh was a diversion.

"What's on the agenda for tomorrow?" Sam was holding her close to his chest, gently running his fingers up and down her back. She loved when he did this.

"I'm going to New York, remember?"

"Ah, work. I forgot."

She wished she could forget, too. She was dreading the long drive with nothing to look forward to in the end but three fourteen-hour days at the clinic. "My patients are counting on me."

She said it to remind herself, more than Sam.

"I'll miss you."

Would he really?

He kissed the top of her head. "Now I know how Susan must have felt."

"What do you mean?"

"This time I'm the one left behind. I'm used to being the one who leaves."

Was he really comparing the intimacy of their relationship to the one he'd had with his wife?

Inherent shyness stopped her from asking him that. "Did she ever complain about being a pro ball player's wife?"

"I know she found the long absences hard, but she never played the guilt card. She was very supportive, right from high school. Every home game I could count on her being in the bleachers, cheering me on."

"What about after high school?"

"We got married right away. Susan came with me to Dartmouth College. Whenever possible, she would travel to the out-of-town games. Same after I was drafted by the Reds."

What a nomadic life. Leigh wasn't sure she could have coped. "What about after Josh was born?"

"Susan stopped traveling with me then. We both wanted our son to grow up in a stable environment. So we bought this house and I spent as much time at home as I could, but a professional athlete doesn't have much control over his schedule."

Leigh shifted to her side so she could see his

face. He looked relaxed. The topic didn't seem to be upsetting him. "Do you ever miss baseball?"

His lips twisted in a one-sided smile.

"You seem to avoid watching games. You don't talk about it, either. You must have lots of interesting stories and anecdotes."

He sighed.

"It's guilt, isn't it? You've associated Andrew and Susan's car accident with your ball career. But, Sam, you have to know that's not fair."

"Fair or not, I'm not the only one who feels that way."

He had to be talking about Kate. "Your sister loves you. She wouldn't want you to be blaming yourself for that."

"Not consciously, no." He rolled over to his back. "Anyway, this isn't just about my sister and the accident. When I see a glimpse of a game on television, or a photograph on the sports page, I can't help thinking of Susan and Josh and all the family time I missed."

She ran a hand over his shoulder, down the corded muscles of his arm. "Are you a lefty?"

"Yes."

"Your muscles are still bigger on this side." She touched a bulging bicep. "As for Susan, at least she had a husband part of the time."

Until she'd met Sam, Leigh rarely regretted not having one herself. She wondered if Susan had known how lucky she was, to be loved so completely.

What Sam and Susan had shared was real. And suddenly Leigh felt like an imposter, not even worthy of the guest bedroom, let alone the master.

"I'd better get a move on. I have a long drive ahead of me tomorrow." Gently she disengaged from Sam's embrace. As she walked toward the bathroom, she waited for Sam's usual invitation to spend the night.

Only this time, it didn't come.

THE DAY AFTER Leigh left, Sam decided to update the photographs on display in his house. He had some current pictures of himself and Josh, a nice studio shot of Kate and Robin from last Christmas. He put out the new pictures, stored some of the old ones in boxes. In the end, there were still pictures of Susan on display—but not as many.

He kept to his running schedule, though it was difficult to motivate himself without Leigh. At the end of his Tuesday run, he wanted to avoid going home to his empty house, so he stopped in to visit his sister.

"Got any chores that need doing?"

He adjusted her temperamental garage door opener, then mowed her extensive lawn. When he was done, Kate had dinner waiting.

"Robin's going to be so glad he doesn't have to mow the lawn this week." She scooped servings of rice and stir-fried chicken onto his plate.

"Speaking of the kid, where is he?"

"Out with friends." Kate joined him at the table with her own plate. She looked at him speculatively. "I can't remember the last time we had dinner, just the two of us."

"It's going to happen more often now. Josh is in his own place and serious about a girl. Robin's growing up, too." The changes were inevitable, but that didn't make them any easier.

"What about Leigh? Can you see her being part of your future?"

"That's a tough one." On many levels their relationship was developing wonderfully. Yet on an emotional plane she was still holding back. Lately he'd been wondering if he might be guilty of doing the same.

"I like her, if my endorsement matters."

He reached across the table to pat her hand. "It does matter." He loved his sister, but he wasn't going to talk about the details of his and Leigh's relationship. "I've been thinking of doing some spring cleaning at the house while she's in New York."

"Oh?"

"I need new sheets. Where do you get things like sheets and towels and such?"

"You can buy them over the Internet." She recited the Web address for a popular department store. "The important thing with sheets is thread count. The higher the better."

That night Sam went online and ordered new bedding for both the master and the spare bedrooms. While he was at it he bought new towels. Big, white towel sheets to replace the powder blue ones Susan had chosen that were now fraying at the edges. He paid extra for express mailing, then hit the submit button.

He went to bed around midnight and thought about Leigh. He'd wondered if she would phone him while she was away, but so far she hadn't.

Out of sight, out of mind?

Or maybe she was just too busy. Well, he was busy, as well, but he could have found time to call her. If he only had her number.

Poor excuse. It reminded him of the string of circumstances that had kept Andrew and Leigh from contacting one another after their summer together.

He reached for his receiver and dialed long

distance directory. A minute later, the phone was ringing. Someone picked up.

"Hello?" Leigh sounded wary.

"You never write. You never call."

She laughed. "Hi, Sam."

Hearing her laugh, the familiar way she said his name, he was very glad he'd made the effort to find her number. "So how's it going?"

"It's been tough. The drive on Monday seemed very long and I had several major treatments at work today. A root canal, two crowns and an ugly extraction. Plus, a cute little girl who howled every time I went near her."

"So where are you now?"

She hesitated. "In bed."

"Me, too." He took in a deep breath. "Wish you were here with me."

She didn't say anything for the longest time. He worried he'd pushed her too far. But finally, she whispered back. "Me, too."

Sam smiled. "Kate's having a family dinner on Sunday. Can I tell her you'll be there?"

"Of course."

"I'll want to see you before then, though. When do you think you'll be back?"

"Friday night."

"Come straight to my place."

"I don't think that's a good idea. It'll be late."

"So?"

"And I've already called Kate, so she's expecting me at the inn."

He didn't want her to stay at the inn at all. He wanted her with him. And soon. "What about Saturday?"

"We could meet for a run."

It wasn't running he had in mind, but he supposed it would make a good start. Especially when he considered the way they usually cooled off…

SATURDAY MORNING, before meeting Sam for their run, Leigh went to visit her daughter. The afternoon was warm and they sat out on the front porch. Leigh thought her daughter looked great. And so grown up.

Taylor was wearing a full skirt and simple tank top, sandals and very little makeup. Her skin was looking better every time Leigh saw her.

"So how was the drive?" Taylor asked.

They were sipping iced tea, looking over a view of tree-covered hills. In the autumn, the colors would be fabulous.

"Brutal," Leigh said, frankly. Driving was still foreign to her. In that respect, she remained a big-city woman. But it had been worth all those hours behind the wheel to get here. She'd felt so alone in New York, even though she'd called several of her friends and had put in long hours at work.

"You could have stayed home, you know. I'm fine, Mom. I really am."

"You look wonderful," Leigh conceded.

"Thanks. So do you." Taylor's eyes gleamed. "I hear that you and Josh's dad have been enjoying running together."

"Sam is very athletic."

"I'll bet."

"Taylor! Don't look at me that way. I'm your mother—"

"I know, but that doesn't mean you can't have some fun for a change. I'm *glad*, Mom. Really."

"You don't find it uncomfortable? That I'm seeing the father of your boyfriend?" It was so strange to be having this conversation with her daughter. And yet it felt good, to be getting her relationship with Sam out in the open.

"It's fine, Mom," Taylor reassured her. "I think Josh's dad is great."

Well, they had that in common, at least. "Okay. Enough of that, then. Tell me how your work is going. Are you enjoying the event-planning business?"

Taylor broke eye contact. "It's fine." She pumped a little more enthusiasm into her voice. "I've been working on party favors for an anniversary dinner. When Josh gets back from his meeting we're going to decorate the hall for the big event."

"Great," Leigh said, trying to force some enthusiasm into her voice, too. She'd seen the favors when she'd first arrived…little silk flowers attached to small boxes of chocolates. Putting together a dozen of the confections might be fun. Doing a hundred, as Taylor needed to do, seemed like a tedious job.

"As long as you're happy," Leigh added.

"Oh, I am."

"And things with Josh…they're good, too?"

Taylor nodded. "He's a real sweetie."

"Okay, then. I guess I should get going. I need to change before I meet Sam at two for our run. I'll see you at Kate's dinner tomorrow?"

"You bet."

Taylor walked her to her car, then waved goodbye before heading back to the cottage. Before driving off, Leigh took a moment to watch as her daughter disappeared.

Taylor had never looked better and she said everything was going well, but something didn't seem quite right.

There'd been a slight hesitation before some of Taylor's responses. And her eyes. While she'd looked at Leigh directly several times, she hadn't been able to hold the gaze for long.

Was it Sam and the fact that her mother was involved with him? Or was it something else? Leigh knew there was something bothering her daughter. She only wished Taylor trusted her enough to tell her what it was.

SAM CALLED Leigh shortly after she'd returned to the inn. She was sitting on the end of the bed, looking out over her view.

Her view. She was becoming quite proprietorial about this turret room of Kate's.

"So are you up for our run?"

"Definitely."

"I've been training," Sam warned her. "I'm going to run your ass off."

"We'll see about that." She'd managed to get only one run in during the five days she'd been gone. Still, she thought she would still be able to keep up, if not set the pace, as usual.

Leigh changed and drove to the designated trail where she and Sam had arranged to meet. Though she was ten minutes early, he was already there.

He took her hands, kissed her on the lips. "I missed you."

The simple words took her breath away, but though she'd felt the same way about him, she made no similar admission.

They ran seven miles and, as Sam had promised, he'd grown stronger and faster in just the week they'd been apart.

Later, they went to his house. On the drive over, all Leigh could think about was how his hands were going to feel on her body. She'd grown addicted to his touch, to the sweetness of his kisses and the mixture of passion and tenderness in their lovemaking.

Was she just making up for lost time…all those years when she hadn't had time, or hadn't *made* time, for men in her life?

Or was there something special about Sam? Special about the two of them together?

She couldn't stop watching him as he moved around the house. Getting her a drink of water, then opening a bottle of wine and pulling out two crystal glasses.

Usually they had juice after a run. "This is special."

"Yeah. It is." He touched his glass to hers. "Like I said…I missed you."

She'd missed him, too. So much. And now he was making her feel things she'd never felt before. Wanted. Cherished.

He left no doubt in her mind when he kissed her the next time. After several long, delicious minutes, she was clinging to him.

"Come to my room," he whispered, and she was surprised to see that this time it was *his* room he took her to, and not the spare room across the hall.

It was a nice room, with a few family photos on the bureau...none of Susan, surprisingly. The bedspread was a chocolate brown and looked new. The sheets underneath were scrumptiously soft Egyptian cotton.

After they made love, they drank more wine sitting in the family room. Here, Leigh noticed more changes. A new picture on the wall. A different throw over the sofa. Fresh candles on the coffee table.

He'd spruced up the place, gently eliminating the constant reminders of his dead wife.

He'd left a few things. There was still one cross-stitch in the hallway and a couple of Susan's photos remained in the collage on the entertainment unit.

Leigh studied Sam's face. He was following

the movie on the television, but she knew he was aware that he was being watched.

"You didn't do this for me, did you?"

He shifted position, then gave her a quick glance. "What if I did?"

She didn't know what to say. The idea that he had made all these changes for her was flattering, but also frightening. His every touch, his every kiss, told her that she mattered to him.

But this really cinched it.

Why her? After six years, why was he going to all this effort for her? Surely there were other women, other possibilities? For a man like Sam, there always would be.

Could it be that there really was something special between them?

Her heart raced at the idea. She turned to the TV screen, but couldn't focus on a thing.

Were she and Sam falling in love with each other? And if they were, what the hell was she going to do about it?

WHEN SAM AWOKE the next morning, Leigh was still beside him. He watched her for a moment. In her sleep she looked beautiful, impossibly young...and happy.

He'd missed her enough when she was gone

that he'd found himself thinking about the future. He hadn't done much of that since Susan's accident. Getting through each day, one at a time, had been enough at the beginning. Over the years, pain had dulled to sadness and gradually to contentment.

He'd been grateful for that, and grateful for what he still had in his life. People to love and to look after. His son, his sister and his nephew. They had become his focus.

He'd never imagined falling in love again. Getting remarried. Certainly, from the outside, Leigh Hartwell didn't seem like the type to change his mind about that.

And yet, unaccountably, she'd done exactly that.

He was challenged by her and, at the same time, desperately attracted to her. He craved her company and her conversation. More than anything, though, he was drawn to the softness he sensed at her core. The vulnerability she'd trained herself to hide.

The more she learned to trust him, the more he saw of that side of her. And the more deeply his feelings for her grew.

For the first time in six years he saw a different sort of future for himself. One that he could share with a woman by his side.

He had a hard time imagining himself in New York City, though. He loved this valley and he felt an obligation to Kate, not to mention Robin and Josh. The boys were growing up, but they still needed a male presence in their lives.

Would Leigh consider selling her practice in the city and setting up shop here?

It would help if her daughter ended up staying in Jefferson permanently, but what if she didn't?

He'd tried to have a talk with his son the other day. It hadn't gone well. Josh had been reluctant to discuss his relationship with Taylor at all, but the little he'd said had given Sam the impression that the relationship wasn't working out as smoothly as before.

Josh had seemed overwhelmed, in fact, by how quickly their relationship had progressed, which reinforced Sam's suspicion that Taylor's decision to postpone university and move in with Josh had been made rashly, out of rebellion against her mother.

Josh had been infatuated enough to go along with her, but would those feelings last?

Now that Leigh was no longer pushing to break them apart, the kids might question for themselves whether they'd moved in together too quickly.

For their sake, Sam hoped they would. At the same time he worried about the impact that would have on his and Leigh's relationship. If Taylor decided to move back to New York, he had no doubt that Leigh would follow.

CHAPTER FIFTEEN

FOR THE NEXT FEW weeks, Leigh concentrated on
her running, spending time with Sam and meeting
her daughter occasionally for lunch or an ice
cream. She still had the sense that something was
bothering Taylor, but she didn't push.

Taylor seemed to be regretting her decision
not to go to college. Every time they met, Leigh
prayed Taylor would tell her she'd changed her
mind. So far she hadn't, but Leigh hoped she
would soon.

On the second Sunday in August Sam and
Leigh ran twenty miles. It was the second longest
run they would have before their marathon.

And it practically killed them.

When they reached the end, Sam opened the
tailgate of his truck and they sat on that, drinking
water, soaking up the afternoon sun.

"We did it. Good work, Sam." She couldn't
believe he had built to this distance so quickly.

"I couldn't have done it without you."

She thought he probably could, but it was nice that he gave her the credit. She took in his lean physique. He'd shed some weight since they'd started running. His muscles were more taut and defined. He looked hot.

She glanced away, too tired to go there right now.

"Hey." He took her hand. "I saw that look. You were checking me out."

She smiled. "I was just thinking that if you keep losing weight, those new jeans you finally ordered aren't going to fit anymore."

"I'll cinch my belt in a notch." He brought her hand to his mouth, kissed it, then moved a little closer. "Those last two miles were hell, but I feel great now."

"It's a wonderful feeling of accomplishment, isn't it?"

"I wasn't talking about the running. I was talking about you. Being with you always feels right. Have you noticed that, too?"

"Yes," she agreed cautiously, worried about where this conversation was headed.

"Leigh, I think I'm—"

Before he could say it, she leaned over to kiss him. His mouth was cool from the water, but she soon heated him up.

He stroked the back of her head, angled his mouth for a deeper kiss. A few minutes later, he pulled gently away. "Back to my place?"

More times than not, they showered there after their runs. Then they made love and ended up in the shower, again. But the longer run today had put them behind schedule.

"I'm not sure. Don't we have dinner at Kate's?"

He sighed. "Yeah. And I need to marinate the meat. I'm on barbecue duty, as usual."

She brushed the side of his face with her hand. "We'd better skip our post-run workout this time, then."

"You're probably right."

Sam drove her back to the inn, where she took a short nap, then showered and dressed.

Later, she entered the stats from their run into her log. She was really pleased with their times. If they kept up this pace on race day they'd have no trouble bringing in the marathon at three and a half hours.

That was as far into the future as Leigh would allow herself to think these days. The marathon. She'd be living in the city by then, but at least the race would give her and Sam a reason to see each other again.

After that…who knew?

During dinner, Leigh could sense Sam watching her. When they'd finished their run today he'd almost told her he loved her. She'd stopped him with a kiss, but that wasn't always going to work. One of these days he was actually going to say those words. And she had no idea what to say in return.

She was pretty sure she loved him, too. But until Taylor's life was back on track, she couldn't think about what that meant. Would Sam move to New York to be with her? She doubted it.

Could she move here, for him?

She'd have to sell out of her business, leave her partners and friends behind. Maybe it would be worth it, if what she and Sam had was real. How could she be sure that it was? And what about their kids? For her, Taylor had to come first and she knew Sam felt the same about Josh.

Her daughter seemed quiet tonight and for the first time that Leigh could remember, she and Josh weren't sitting beside one another at the dinner table.

Leigh looked from one to the other, trying to gauge their moods. Had they had a disagreement? Both Josh and Taylor's expressions were unreadable, however.

Kate and Sam had been talking about local

issues for some time, when Robin shifted the conversation to baseball. He'd invited a friend to dinner and he and Evan had been watching the Red Sox play earlier that afternoon.

"It was an amazing game, Uncle Sam."

"Yeah," Evan agreed. "They got out of a jam with two pickoffs in the seventh inning."

"Impressive," Sam murmured.

"But nothing could ever beat the time you got three in one inning," Robin pointed out.

"Really?" Evan stopped eating. "When did that happen?"

Everyone fell silent and looked at Sam. Leigh leaned forward, curious to see if he would add anything. Usually when the subject of baseball came up Sam could be counted on to make an excuse and leave the room.

This time, though, he stayed where he was. When he looked at her, she smiled encouragingly. "What's a pickoff?"

"When a pitcher catches one of the runners off base."

"And you did that three times?"

"In one inning," Robin elaborated. "Uncle Sam had just been called up from the minors by the Reds. I wasn't even born yet, but I've seen it on TV. He was incredible."

"What happened?" she asked Sam.

Everyone in the room was looking at him. Leigh could tell they expected him to brush off her question.

Instead, he cleared his throat. "Like Robin said, it was my first game in the big leagues. The plan was to break me in slowly, but the game went into extra innings and our team was struggling."

"Their pitcher walked the first three hitters leading off the seventeenth inning," Robin elaborated. "The manager had to do something."

Sam nodded. "So I found myself called in for my first big league game with the bases loaded and none out…"

SAM'S STORY about three pickoffs in one inning led to another story, and then another. Leigh was fascinated and so were Robin and his friend. As for Sam, his joy for the sport came out stronger with each anecdote. So much so, that soon Kate and Josh were sharing in the remembrances.

Leigh had to wonder why he'd kept all that passion bottled inside of him for so many years.

And why he'd decided to let it out now.

Was it because of her?

The warmth in Sam's eyes when he looked at

her made her think yes. So did the changes he'd made to his house, his new clothes, the way he casually included her when talking about the future.

As the baseball talk tapered off, Leigh noticed her daughter check the time on her watch. She'd seemed distracted all meal and hadn't contributed to the conversation one bit.

When Sam stood and started stacking dishes, Leigh hurried to stop him. "Sit down and relax. You and Kate did the cooking so Taylor and I are washing dishes."

Taylor looked as if she wanted to object, but as Leigh had calculated, good manners won out. She joined her mother in the kitchen, after extracting a promise from Josh that he would play just one more video game with Robin and Evan and then they would leave.

Leigh ran a sink of soapy water and started washing. Once they were alone in the kitchen she asked quietly, "Is everything okay?"

Taylor took the clean casserole dish out of her hands and rinsed away the bubbles. "Sure."

"You seem a little quiet."

"I'm tired. Josh and I had to work Friday and Saturday night on the party for the historical society."

They talked about that for a while, then Leigh told her about the run. "We went twenty miles today. I think we might actually finish that marathon in September."

"Wow."

There was a marked lack of enthusiasm in her daughter's voice. "Are you sure you're just tired?"

No answer.

Leigh wiped her hands, then turned to face her daughter. Taylor kept drying dishes, avoiding her gaze.

A tear ran down her face, then another.

"Oh, Taylor. What's wrong? Is it Josh?"

Tears were falling in a steady stream now. Taylor stopped the pretense of drying dishes and balled the tea towel in her hands.

When Leigh put an arm over her shoulders, Taylor stiffened, but didn't pull away. "Did you have an argument?"

"N-no."

"But something's wrong between you," Leigh guessed.

Taylor let out a quiet sob. Leigh opened her arms and sighed with relief when her daughter turned into them.

"I-I think Josh is sorry he ever invited me to Jefferson."

"Did he say that?"

"Well…no. But I can tell."

Much as she wanted the relationship between her daughter and Josh to end, Leigh couldn't take any satisfaction from her daughter's obvious pain. "Have you tried talking to him?"

"I-I'm scared."

"It takes courage to talk about the important stuff," Leigh acknowledged, feeling like a hypocrite as she said it. "But you need to be honest with one another. Tell him how you're feeling. Ask him about his feelings, too."

Taylor choked out a laugh. "I can't believe you're saying this. I was sure you'd have my bags packed for New York if I admitted I was having problems with Josh."

In truth, that was exactly what Leigh wanted to do. "Maybe I've changed."

Taylor's arms tightened around her neck. "Oh, Mom. I'm just so scared."

That was the second time she'd said that. Suddenly Leigh wondered if this was about more than just Josh. She pulled back and studied her daughter's reddened eyes.

"Taylor?"

Her daughter held on tighter.

It couldn't be, Leigh told herself. She'd had so

many talks with her daughter. Taylor was too smart to make such a big mistake as—

"Mom? I think I might be pregnant."

CHAPTER SIXTEEN

FOR A LONG MOMENT Leigh couldn't breathe. She
couldn't think. Her arms dropped to her sides and
she heard a roaring in her ears. She felt as if she'd
been grabbed by an undertow and sucked into the
depths of the ocean.

*I knew it. I knew it. I never should have trusted
you to go on that vacation.*

Were those her words or her mother's?

It didn't matter. They were true.

Taylor, her beautiful, smart, *young* daughter,
was pregnant.

She never should have trusted Taylor. Or Josh.
Or Sam. They'd all said that she was being
overprotective, that she needed to let go a little.

But what did a couple of teenagers know about
the world? She was the mother, she should have
made sure her daughter was protected…in every
sense of the word.

"I knew it."

Now her mother's words and hers were the same. Just as her mistake had become her daughter's.

"Mom?"

Taylor's voice sounded far away. As the roaring subsided and Leigh recovered her focus, she was surprised to see that her daughter was still standing right beside her.

She wouldn't lose her temper. She wouldn't say *I told you so*.

She would be calm.

"It's okay, Taylor. We can take care of this. I know a good doctor. We'll take you to the city and find out our options and everything will be fine."

It was a lie. Everything was going to be different now. Taylor didn't know how a pregnancy could change a young woman's life, but Leigh did.

"I'm not sure I want to go to the city. I'm sure they have good doctors here."

"Well, yes. But don't you think it would be better to be on home turf? We'll stop by the cottage and you can pack your bags."

"I haven't even told Josh, yet. I haven't even— Oh, never mind. I don't know why I told you this. I should have known you'd go ballistic."

"How can you say that? I'm perfectly calm."
Her insides might be quivering like gelatin, but
she was doing her best not to show it.

"Yeah. Calm. That's a laugh. You'd like
nothing better than for me to be an absolute
disaster so that you could step in and save me.
But this isn't your problem, Mom. It's mine and
Josh's. Unlike you, I intend to include the father
of my baby in my decision."

Leigh winced. "Of course you'll talk to Josh.
I wasn't suggesting otherwise. I still think that returning to the city—"

"Not going to happen, Mom." Taylor glared as
she swiped the tears from her face.

"This is no time to act like a temperamental
toddler."

Taylor rolled her eyes to the ceiling. "I can't
believe it. I thought you'd *changed*."

"And I thought I could trust you." Sam had convinced her that she could, that she *should*. "You
kept telling me you were old enough to make your
own decisions. That you were an adult now."

Why had she listened to her? Damn it, she'd
known better. "Taylor, please listen to me this time.
If we head back to the city tonight I'll pull some
strings and we'll get into the doctor by tomorrow.
We'll take this one step at a time and—"

"No! Mom, I won't do it."

How dare Taylor yell at *her?* Was any of this *her* fault? "Please don't raise your voice. Do you want—"

Sam appeared in the doorway and Leigh shut her mouth.

"Is everything okay?"

She and Taylor glared at each other.

"Leigh?" he asked, again.

She shook her head at him, backing away when he tried to step closer to her. "We're having a private conversation here. If you don't mind—"

But Josh appeared next and as soon as she saw him, Taylor ran to him. "We have to go. Now."

"Taylor. Don't you dare walk out of this room." Leigh put all the authority she could muster into her voice, but her daughter didn't even glance back at her and neither did Josh. If those two had been having troubles you couldn't tell it now. Arms linked, they disappeared down the hall and a moment later Leigh heard the front door open and close.

For a long moment there was silence in the room. Leigh struggled to comprehend what had happened.

Taylor had walked out on her.

Taylor was in trouble and she didn't want her

mother to help her. She wanted Josh. An under-employed boy she'd known for less than two months.

"What the hell was that about?"

Leigh turned to Sam. In that moment, all her frustration and anger and worry boiled over.

"Taylor's pregnant," she told him. "I hope you're happy."

SAM STARED at Leigh a long time. He'd been so hopeful tonight. He'd felt like a kid again, passionate about life and about his future. It took a minute for the meaning of Leigh's words to sink in.

Taylor pregnant?

"That can't be right." Josh knew better. The importance of birth control had been drilled into that kid.

"It isn't right. But, unfortunately, it's the truth."

Fury radiated out of every one of Leigh's pores. The way she was glaring at him, Sam could tell she held him responsible.

For a moment he felt a father's anger and disappointment. Josh knew better, damn it.

But this wasn't the time for those feelings. Leigh looked like she was ready to erupt and he didn't want it happening in his sister's kitchen.

"Come on. Let's get out of here." He grabbed Leigh's hand and led her to the sliding doors. He'd make his apologies to Kate later.

A light wind carried the fragrances from his sister's flower garden as Sam led Leigh around the yard to the front drive. He stopped short when he saw that Josh had taken his truck.

Leigh noticed the missing vehicle at the same time. "How did he get the keys?"

"I left them in the ignition. I always do."

She looked at him like he was nuts.

"This isn't New York City."

"No kidding." She yanked her hand from his, then kept walking toward her own car.

It took him a moment to realize what she was up to. "There's no point following them."

"What do you suggest? Leaving them alone? Trusting them to make the right decision on their own?"

He said nothing.

"Forget it, Sam. I tried your approach. It didn't work."

"And you think racing after them and arguing and fighting will?"

"You know what I think? You're afraid to confront your son. Afraid to tell him he's done something wrong. There is such a thing as being too lenient with your children, Sam."

"Hey. What gives you the right—"

Leigh laughed harshly. "So you can criticize my parenting skills but yours are off-limits?"

She had a point, but he wasn't in the mood to concede it. "Please, give me your keys. Let's go for a walk. We need to cool down."

"Practicing your perfect parent skills on me now, Sam? Well, I'm sorry, but I'm not impressed. Sometimes a parent has to set limits. If you'd charged Josh rent for that cottage—"

"He can't afford that, and you know it."

"That's exactly the point. If our kids want us to treat them like adults, then they need to behave like them. Paying your rent is part of being a responsible adult."

"What does that have to do with Taylor being pregnant?"

"All I'm saying is that she shouldn't have been shacked up in the cabin with your son in the first place."

She opened the car door and climbed into the driver's seat. He ran after her, just managing to open the passenger door and slide inside before she drove off.

"Okay. I've made mistakes," he told her. "Let's

not compound them. There'll be plenty of time for talking in the morning once everyone's had a chance to cool off."

She wouldn't look at him. Wouldn't say another word. After a few minutes he gave up. He stared off to the side feeling sick to his stomach.

Things had been going so well. Now this. Suddenly his future was blacker than the view out the window.

"SHOULDN'T WE ASK your dad before we take his truck?" Taylor tried to buckle her seat belt, but her hands were shaking. Josh leaned over from the driver's side to help her.

"He won't mind. Aunt Kate will give him a ride home. Or your mom."

Taylor closed her eyes and sank back into the seat. "Thank you."

"No sweat."

She heard the engine start, felt the bumps as Josh drove down the lane and back onto the highway. She loved the way he'd come to her aid without asking for an explanation. Still, he deserved one.

"Mom really freaked out back there."

"Yeah? I thought things were cool between the two of you."

"They were. But I—" Taylor couldn't finish. Not yet. She didn't know quite what to say.

She'd thought her mother had changed. That she could trust her enough to ask her advice. She hadn't even told Josh, yet.

But now she'd have to.

The thing was…she really didn't want to. She and Josh had had so much fun at first. But lately she'd been missing her friends. She'd been thinking of Cornell, too, and had even gone on the Web site a few times to look at the course offerings.

Josh was getting tired of having her live with him, as well, she guessed. He was too polite to say anything, but lately he'd been spending more time on his video games. She'd overheard one of his friends complaining that he never hung out with them anymore.

Josh had sounded kind of trapped when he'd said, "I know. Sorry."

Imagine how trapped he'd feel when he heard this.

"Josh?"

"Yeah."

A few raindrops hit the windshield. Then a bunch more. Josh turned the wiper switch and the rubber blades squeaked over the glass.

"I missed my period this month."

She felt the truck jerk a little to one side. Maybe telling him while he was driving hadn't been such a smart idea. But at least this way they had an excuse not to look at one another.

"Um…that's not good, right?"

"No. It's not good." She stared at the wipers, at the arcs they cut through what was now a steady rain. She supposed Josh was thinking, like her, about the time when he'd run out of condoms and they'd tried the withdrawal method.

Josh had sucked at the withdrawal method.

"Is that why your mom hit the roof?"

"I don't know why I told her." Actually, she did know why. She'd been hoping that her mother would say something like, *Oh, I miss my periods all the time. It doesn't necessarily mean anything.*

She'd wanted to be reassured. But she should have known better than to look for that reassurance from her mother. Unplanned pregnancy was her hot button.

And, boy, had Taylor pressed it good, tonight.

"She'll probably come after us," Josh guessed.

Taylor sighed. "Yes. She wants me to go back to the city and see our doctor."

"You could do that. Or…we have doctors here, too."

"That's what I told her. But I'd like to make sure I'm pregnant first."

"Have you bought one of those drugstore kits?"

"No." Again, she was scared. She was only eighteen. She really didn't want a baby. "I know I have to."

"We'll buy one together, first thing in the morning." Josh slowed the truck as they approached home. He pulled into the lane and parked in his dad's usual spot. When Taylor didn't get out of the truck, he turned to look at her.

"Want to go inside?"

"Not really," she confessed. "I'm guessing Mom will be about fifteen minutes behind us."

"We could always take off. I don't have any appointments for the next few days."

She liked that idea. "But where would we go? We don't have enough money for a hotel or anything."

"That's true. But I have another idea. Let's see if we can find the key to Dad's garage."

IT WAS RAINING steadily when Leigh parked behind Sam's truck ten minutes after leaving Kate's. She left the keys in the ignition and stepped straight into a puddle.

Damn. She shook the water from her foot, then headed for the cottage, her strides long and determined. Sam didn't follow, but that was okay. She didn't need his support. She knew what she had to do.

Taylor had caught her off guard earlier. She'd reacted out of fear and anger. During the drive, though, Leigh had had a chance to mull things over. She'd thought about the way she had felt when she'd been in this exact situation.

Scared. Alone. Worried.

Well, Taylor wasn't going to go through all the anguish she'd endured. She had to let her daughter know that she was here for her. That she'd support whatever decision she and Josh made.

Josh. It stung to realize that he would be a part of the decision-making process, but Taylor was right, he ought to be.

Just as Drew should have been eighteen years ago.

Taylor was right to be angry with her about that, too. Because of Leigh's thoughtless decision, her daughter would never have a chance to meet her father or get to know him.

She stepped up onto the creaky wooden porch, then rapped her fist against the old door. As she waited for someone to respond, she looked back just as Sam disappeared inside his garage.

She'd been so angry at him earlier. Now, she didn't know what to think. She still thought he was too lenient with his son. But was this situation really his fault?

No. She'd gone too far with that one.

She knocked a second time and only then did it register that the cottage was dark except for a dim light in the entranceway. The kids weren't here.

She jogged back to the parked vehicles. The door to Sam's garage was open and he was just standing there. "What are you doing?"

"Josh's van is missing."

She scanned the yard. Sam was right. She hadn't even thought to check.

Now what was she going to do?

Suddenly aware of how drenched she was getting, she stepped inside the garage with Sam. A motorboat took up most of the space, but there were also bikes and a kayak in here. The shelves were filled with smaller sporting equipment and tools—the usual garage stuff. Sam seemed to be fascinated by the shelving unit on the side wall.

It was empty.

She wrapped her arms around her chest,

feeling chilled. Sam was close enough to notice. If this were happening just a few hours before she'd lashed out at him, he would be putting his arm around her right now and offering her comfort.

She couldn't worry about that, though. Taylor was her first priority.

"I wonder where they went?"

Sam still said nothing.

"I hope they're back soon. I won't be able to sleep until I talk to them."

"Well, I wouldn't expect them before tomorrow," Sam said, finally. "They've taken the camping gear."

CHAPTER SEVENTEEN

LEIGH SPREAD the map of the White Mountains over Sam's kitchen table. He'd just gotten off the phone with his sister, trying to explain—without mentioning the fact that Taylor might be pregnant—why they'd deserted the dinner party so abruptly and without saying goodbye.

"Can you show me where they might be headed?" she asked.

What had possessed them to take off camping in the driving rain? According to the forecast, the rain was going to continue all night. They'd be soaked by morning. Tired and miserable.

It wouldn't make for clearheadedness on anyone's part.

"There are lots of possibilities." Sam was being very polite and distant. Under the circumstances, Leigh couldn't ask for more.

"Do you and Josh camp very often?"

"All the time."

"Could you show me some of your favorite places?"

Sam raised his eyebrows, then took the pen from her hand and circled seven spots. "Those are just the close ones. If they decide to drive for more than an hour, they could end up anywhere. There are tons of great campgrounds in the White Mountains."

That was disheartening. But maybe she'd be lucky.

"I'll try the close ones first." She folded the map accordion-style, then put it in her purse.

"I hate to ask this, but are you planning on leaving right now?"

"Of course."

He let out a long breath, then splayed his hands on the kitchen table. "You aren't going to find them. Even if you do, they won't listen to anything you say. Stay home and keep dry. They'll be back."

Standard Sam advice. "That's what you said when Taylor wanted to stay the weekend. Then again when she decided to abandon her plans for college and move in with Josh. You said if I gave her some space, she would come to her senses."

He crossed his arms over his chest.

"Your approach wasn't very successful, was it, Sam?"

"Maybe not. But do you honestly think there

was anything we could have done that would have changed this? Hell, Leigh, mistakes happen. That's life."

"Is that the best you can offer me? Mistakes happen?"

"Look, maybe I have been too lenient with Josh. If you want to believe that makes me responsible for this situation, then go right ahead. It still doesn't make any sense for you to go out in this storm when you have absolutely no idea where the kids went."

"My child is out there, Sam. Pregnant, angry and confused. Neither she nor Josh is capable of thinking straight. What if they leave the state? What if they decide to get married?"

"It's out of our hands."

"No, it isn't. I'm going after them." She hesitated, then decided she had to ask. "Will you come with me?"

Seconds ticked by as Sam stared across the room at her. Finally, he shook his head. "No, Leigh. I won't."

She took a deep breath and gave him one last look. He was such a handsome man—strong, protective and honorable. He was the sort of man she'd imagined would do anything to help someone he loved.

So why wouldn't he help her now?

IT WAS STILL RAINING when Leigh left Jefferson an hour later with her hastily packed suitcase tossed into the trunk.

Sam should have been in the seat next to her. He should have been *helping* her. And the fact that he wasn't told her everything she needed to know about the status of their relationship.

It was over.

Rain pummeled her car with the sort of steady, unhurried rhythm that could go on for hours, or days.

She should be worrying about her daughter, out in this bad weather with only a tent and an old van for protection.

Instead, she thought of Sam, of the slump in his shoulders as he'd watched her leave. She thought of the new sheets on his bed and the fire in his eyes as he'd warmed to the telling of his old baseball stories only hours ago.

Leigh could feel the muscles in her neck tighten and harden. She held her head stiffly as the sound of the rain echoed around her. The dark, wet highway glistened ahead, a black path leading her through an unknown world of mountains and trees.

In this weather, at this time of night, she could easily miss a signpost and end up lost, but Leigh didn't consider stopping. The first campground was less than an hour from Jefferson. She checked at the office, but no one had registered that night.

Back in the car, she crossed that site off her list and started to head for the next. Partway there, she saw a turnoff for New York City. She pulled over to the side of the road and tried to gather her thoughts.

What had sounded plausible earlier that night when she'd been studying the map at Sam's place, was now clearly impractical.

She wasn't going to find Taylor and Josh.

Even if she did, Sam was right. They wouldn't listen to her.

Maybe leaving Jefferson hadn't been about finding Taylor after all. Maybe it had just been about leaving Jefferson.

Because it was time.

HER MANHATTAN APARTMENT felt cold and empty when Leigh let herself in at six o'clock in the morning. Her neck was now rigid, the muscles clenched from hours of late-night driving. She sorted through the phone messages, but none were from Taylor or Sam.

She spent a restless couple of hours in her own bed, then showered and dressed and walked to the clinic. "Hi, Steph," she greeted the receptionist.

"Leigh?" Steph, who'd been with them since

they'd opened ten years ago, efficiently scrolled down the computer screen in front of her. "Were we expecting you? I don't see any appointments."

"I'm back early. I'll catch up on paperwork today. If you could get some of my patients in for tomorrow, though, that would be great."

"So you're full-time again?"

"Full-time," she agreed. In the back office, she grabbed a coffee, then signed in to her computer. She'd just opened her e-mail account when Wenda appeared.

"So it's true. You're back." She slung a long leg over the stool next to Leigh's workstation.

Leigh turned from a message from one of her patient's insurance companies and studied her friend. "You changed your hairstyle."

Wenda fingered the blond spikes on the top of her head. "I could have gone gray, you've been away so long."

"Thanks for covering for me. I know it meant extra work for everyone."

"That's okay. We all love Taylor, too. How did you talk her into dumping the new guy and getting her butt to Cornell?"

Leigh had sworn she wouldn't return to work until Taylor was safely in college. Since she was here a week early, of course Wenda assumed it was because Taylor was where she was supposed to be.

She'd have to confess the truth, eventually. But not yet.

"It's a long story."

"Want to go for drinks later?"

"That sounds good."

"Maybe we should go for a run first?"

"But it's Monday." And their group usually went out on Tuesday and Thursday.

"Didn't you say you were training for a marathon?"

This morning, she'd barely found the energy to drag herself out of bed. Her neck still ached. She couldn't imagine running five miles, let alone twenty-six.

"I'm registered," she admitted. "But I'm thinking of dropping out."

"After training for two months? Come on, Leigh. You've only got another four weeks to go."

Leigh wavered. Could she do it? Without Sam? He'd been with her every step of the way so far. It wouldn't feel right to run the marathon without him.

But she was afraid that nothing was going to feel right anymore. It wasn't just Taylor's absence weighing on her heart.

Sam. What was he doing right now? Had he

thought about her since she'd left? Was he sorry he hadn't come with her after all?

No, or he would have called.

Leigh sighed. She'd pined after Drew for so long when she was younger. She couldn't bear the thought of going through all that pain over Sam.

"I'll help you, Leigh. What's your scheduled distance for today?"

She had her running log memorized. "I'm in week nine of my training. I'm supposed to run twenty miles today."

"I'll run the first ten with you."

Leigh really didn't think she had twenty miles in her, anymore, but she could at least try. Maybe it was possible to outrun heartbreak.

"Okay," she agreed. "Let's do it."

LEIGH FELT BETTER on the run than she'd expected. The first ten miles were a struggle, but she had Wenda's encouragement to keep her going. After that, she hit her stride and she still felt strong at the end of the twenty miles.

All her training must be paying off. She walked to cool off, did a little stretching, then headed for her apartment, stopping at a deli for a take-out sandwich and a tub of coleslaw on the way.

After her shower, she ate ravenously, and only then did she allow herself to check her messages.

Nothing.

A week went by. Finally, on Sunday afternoon, she came home from a run to find a recording from Sam.

Heart pounding, she sank to the floor, the receiver pressed to her ear.

"Leigh, I thought you should know that the kids are back from their camping trip, safe and sound."

Thank God.

"Turns out they went farther than I expected. They drove all the way to Canada and stayed in the lower townships of Quebec. Taylor will probably be in touch with you soon. She and Josh have been doing a lot of thinking."

And...? Leigh wanted more details, but Sam didn't provide them.

"I hope you're doing okay."

Leigh stretched out her legs. Was she doing okay? She was handling her job. Keeping up the running. Who cared if she felt miserable most of the time?

She waited for something else. Something personal. Something that might indicate that Sam had forgiven her for her outburst. That he didn't think she was a terrible mother. That he still had feelings for her.

But there was nothing left on the recording.

She pressed the repeat button and listened to his message one more time so the words were imprinted in her memory.

Sam had said Taylor would call soon, but after another week went by, Leigh lost hope. There'd been plenty of time for Taylor to cool down since their argument. If she had any intention of getting in touch, she would have done so by now.

Leigh tried not to keep track of the passing weeks. She wondered if Taylor had seen a doctor yet. Had she and Josh made any decisions?

A week before the marathon, her daughter sent a postcard, asking Leigh to box up her possessions and send them to Jefferson. There was a postscript at the bottom. *False alarm. I'm not pregnant.*

CHAPTER EIGHTEEN

LEIGH CALLED HER MOTHER after she'd shipped off Taylor's belongings. She called her sister, too, and they talked for longer than she could ever remember doing. Maybe she needed to make more of an effort with her family than she'd done in the past.

Still, she knew she'd never have the easy camaraderie with her mother and her sister that Sam had with Kate.

On the day before her race, Leigh gassed up the car she'd purchased when she was in Jefferson. It was the first time she'd driven it since she'd returned to the city and she was surprised how good it felt to be behind the wheel of a vehicle again. Once she was on the Interstate, she settled into the four-hour drive. The leaves had begun to change and the colors were beautiful, especially as she neared the Adirondacks.

She arrived at the small resort community of

Schroon Lake in time to check out the route. Already, volunteers were busy putting up signs and erecting the pit stops that would provide welcome hydration and washroom facilities to the runners tomorrow.

Leigh couldn't believe she was really going to do this. She was going to run her first marathon... that is, if she managed to finish. She stopped to stretch her muscles, testing them for strength and flexibility.

She'd been lucky to get through her training without any injuries. Physically, she knew she'd never been stronger. If she was ever going to run a marathon, now was the time.

During the weeks she'd spent training in Jefferson, she'd imagined running this race with Sam beside her and with Taylor cheering her on. Now she had to do it alone. Even Wenda, who had been planning to drive up from New York with her, had had to cancel because of a family emergency.

So there would be no familiar face waiting when she crossed that finish line tomorrow. But it didn't matter. She was running this race for herself, to prove she could do it.

On race day, Leigh awoke before the alarm went off. The inn where she was staying offered a special breakfast for marathoners. She only had a power shake and a banana, afraid to eat more in case her stomach rebelled later.

The inn was full of other runners and all of them were friendly, exuding positive energy. Leigh smiled and chatted with a few of them. Soon she could feel the adrenaline buzz, too.

An hour before the race, she went back to her room to gather everything she needed. It was warm outside, so all she'd wear were her running shorts, a sports bra and tank top. She slicked sports gel under her bra strap and on her inner thighs and arms to prevent chafing. A coating of sunscreen, her sunglasses and a cap, and she was ready.

Leigh took one last look at her cell phone before leaving the room. No missed calls. No messages.

She tossed the phone onto the bed and left.

LEIGH'S NERVES were buzzing by the time she reached the start line. There were so many people here. How many of them would actually finish the race?

She wrote her split times on the inside of the bib, then pinned her race number to her tank top. Since she'd slept well and felt good, she was going to stick to her target time of three hours and thirty minutes.

She looked at her watch. Five minutes to start time. She rechecked her bib, her chip, the small pouch she was carrying with her gel pacs and painkillers.

People were lining up now and she jostled for position among them. The adrenaline was coursing through her now. She took several deep breaths, trying to relax. Once she was running, she knew she'd be okay.

All around her people were being kissed, cheered on and encouraged. Was she the only racer who'd come on her own?

Leigh tried to block out the noise of the crowd. Tuning in to her body, she could almost feel the energy gathering in her muscles.

You can do this, Leigh. You can do this.

The horn sounded and they were off.

The first mile was all about hitting her stride and finding her place amid the other runners. One wave of runners ran out ahead of her. Slowly, others fell back. Leigh checked her watch, resisting the urge to pump up the pace a little. She felt good, but she needed to conserve for the long haul.

By mile three she felt in control. Her body felt good. Nothing was chafing. A woman dressed in lime-green shorts seemed to be running at about her pace. She followed behind the other runner, letting her mind drift into the zone.

She felt good. She felt really good. Her mind was sharp and she found herself mulling over the events of the past three months. Since she'd gone back to the city she'd been so lonely. All that had kept her going was training for this race. She didn't know what she was going to do after this weekend.

Train for another marathon?

And another?

Was she really running with a purpose? Or just running so she didn't have to stand still and take stock of the state of her life?

Since she'd boxed up Taylor's possessions and sent them on the bus to Jefferson, she hadn't heard a word from Taylor. She supposed she was still with Josh, working at the event-planning business and having Sunday dinners with Kate and Robin...and Sam.

Almost every day she fought the urge to phone him. She'd left without apologizing for those things she'd said. But she was afraid that if she called him, if she actually heard his voice and he told her he never wanted to hear from her again, she'd crumble. She was barely keeping herself together as it was.

During those weeks when they'd been together in Jefferson, she'd been happier than she'd ever been before. Sam was a wonderful man. She could easily imagine living her life with him.

She knew now that if he had asked her, she would have left New York for him. The fact that she'd never given him the opportunity to do so was another mistake she'd always regret.

At the half-marathon mark, Leigh stopped for a quick bathroom break and to take on more water. She felt so strong she was tempted to pick up her pace and try for a better time.

No. You'll pay the price later if you do. Keep to the plan, Leigh, keep to the plan.

Half an hour later she was glad that she had. Each mile took more effort now. To keep her focus, she pretended Sam was beside her. She pretended he was struggling, that he wanted to quit.

"You can do it, Sam," she muttered. "Don't give up. You've trained too long."

At the twenty-mile mark, the thing she'd read about so many times happened. She hit the wall. Her legs felt as if they were being poked by a thousand needles. The pain was terrible. She popped a painkiller with a drink of water, then allowed herself to walk for thirty seconds.

God, it felt so good to walk. Maybe she could just finish the twenty-six miles this way. No one would know. Why should she kill herself to meet some arbitrary target? It wasn't as if anyone would be watching for her at the finish line and worrying when she didn't show up at the expected time.

Again she pretended Sam was with her. That he needed her help to keep going. "Come on, Sam. You've got to start running again. Your muscles are going to seize if you don't."

She lifted her foot. Forced a light jog. Hell. She couldn't believe how much it hurt, how quickly her muscles had tightened up on her. Eventually she passed another mile marker. Five miles to go now.

How many times had she run five miles and it had seemed like nothing? Now it felt like an impossible distance.

There'd been spectators on the sidelines before, but now there were more of them. Unbelievably, Leigh heard one of them call her name.

"Leigh! Way to go! You're amazing!"

She whipped her head around. Was that Kate?

Yes, it was. And Robin. They were here, cheering her on.

Oh, hell. She was going to cry. She blinked and

set her jaw and tried hard not to wonder where her daughter was right now.

She rounded a corner and a huge hill rose before her. She swore. "Who put that there?"

She'd seen the hill yesterday, but she'd forgotten all about it until now. God, it was cruel to have to face a hurdle like this so close to the end.

"Keep going," she told herself. "One foot in front of the other. Don't focus on anything else, but one foot in front of the other."

Inside her head a voice was screaming, *stop the pain, just stop the pain.*

She refused to listen.

I can do this. I am fit. I am strong.

She repeated the mantra, over and over in her head. And just as she was about to crest the hill, she heard something that made her heart sing.

"Way to go, Mom! I love you, Mom!"

There was Taylor. She was jumping up and down and waving her arms so Leigh could see her. Too tired to lift her hand in acknowledgment, Leigh just smiled. Her lips were so dry, she could barely manage that.

And then she was on the downhill stretch. Leigh opened up her stride and stretched her protesting muscles. A mile remained and she knew it would be the hardest of her life.

Now with every step she could feel pressure building in her chest. The emotions were building. When she crossed that line, she was going to cry. Damn it, she didn't want to, but she could feel the tears coming, clogging her throat and blurring her vision.

The route snaked to the left and suddenly, above the cheering from the crowd, she could hear the speaker booming out names and times. Round the next corner...and there it was. The finish.

Only seconds away now. She was going to make it. She really was.

People were cheering and clapping, but Leigh's eyes were on the clock. Three hours and twenty-nine minutes. She'd made her target time. She couldn't believe it.

A camera snapped a picture as she crossed the line. Oh, God, thank you, thank you, she could finally stop.

"Leigh!"

Another runner was crossing the finish line behind her. She turned and couldn't believe what she saw.

"Sam?"

The tears came then, and Sam pulled her into a tight hug. They were both so sweaty, lips crusted with dried salt, eyes blurry from the tears, but it didn't matter. They were holding each other up, so tired, so tired.

"You're amazing," Sam whispered.

Her body started to tremble. She held on to him tighter. "I didn't think you'd be here."

"What? And waste all those weeks we spent training?"

"Mom!"

Other people were shouting for their mothers, but Leigh knew that voice. As she scanned the people nearby, Taylor pushed through the crowd, with Josh trailing behind.

"You did it, Mom! Congratulations!"

"Taylor!" Leigh let go of Sam and held her arms out to her daughter. She couldn't believe she was here. Her baby girl had made it to the race.

"I love you, Mom. You were terrific."

"Oh, Taylor." She couldn't say anything else. She wasn't just leaking a few tears now, she was flat-out sobbing. Her legs started shaking, badly.

"You need to sit down."

Sam had been hugging his son. Now he put his arm around her waist and he and Taylor helped her to the sidelines.

Josh held up a camera. "I got some great photos of you crossing the finish line."

"Thanks, Josh." It hurt to sit, so she decided to keep standing. A volunteer gave her a blanket. Another removed the chip from her shoe. Every single cell in her body ached. But the pain was worth it, it really was.

She'd done it. She'd run the marathon.

And, best of all, the people she loved had come out to support her.

CHAPTER NINETEEN

WHEN SAM and Josh offered to get some food,
Leigh was glad for the chance to be alone with her
daughter for a bit.

"You're looking good, honey. How are you
feeling?" Not one harsh or judging word was
going to come out of her mouth today. She was
so happy to see Taylor.

"I'm fine, Mom." Taylor shifted her weight
from one foot to the other. "I'm sorry I didn't get
in touch sooner."

There'd been that postcard asking for her
clothes, the blunt postscript about the pregnancy,
but neither one of them mentioned that.

"How's the business going? Are you still
getting lots of engagements?"

Taylor shrugged. "I'm not working with Josh
anymore. He's taken on a new assistant. And he's
enrolled in community college."

Good for Josh. Leigh was sincerely glad for him. "But what about you?"

"I've…moved."

"Oh?" Leigh felt a frisson of alarm for her daughter. Had they broken up? Had Josh broken her little girl's heart?

"I wasn't ready to be a girlfriend, let alone a *live-in* girlfriend."

Leigh couldn't believe she was saying this. "How about Josh?"

"He wasn't ready, either, though he was too polite to say anything. He felt responsible for talking me into coming to Jefferson in the first place."

Josh really was a good kid. Maybe one day…

Leigh smiled at herself. For months she'd been trying to break these two up, now she was thinking of bringing them together again.

"So what have you been doing?" If Taylor wasn't living with Josh anymore, why hadn't she come home?

Taylor looked a little embarrassed, a little proud. "I'm going to Cornell, Mom."

"You are?"

Her daughter nodded.

"I don't know what to say." This day was turning out to be the most amazing of her life.

"It's okay if you admit you're happy. You *are* happy, right?"

"Oh, honey. Of course I am."

"Good. 'Cause I could really use some of that money you saved for my education…."

SAM AND JOSH returned with some fruit and granola bars. Leigh ate cautiously, worried that her stomach would rebel after hours of gel pacs and sports drinks.

Kate and Robin had found the guys at the food tent. Now Kate was on her cell phone, trying to book a restaurant for a celebratory meal later that night. Robin, Josh and Taylor were walking along the lake, taking in the sights.

All around them people were celebrating, smiling…puking. There was no denying that finishing a marathon was harder on some people than others.

"How are you feeling now, Leigh?" Sam asked.

"Terrible and wonderful, all at the same time." Everything hurt. Her muscles, her skin, her stomach. "I still can't believe we both did it."

She felt anxious as their eyes met. She wasn't sure why he was here, what it meant that he'd still run the race and that he'd sought her out at the finish line. But since he was here, there was something she had to say.

"Sam, I'm sorry I talked to you the way I did that night. And I'm sorry I walked out on you."

"You were in shock. But I did hope that after you had a few days to think things over, I'd hear from you."

"I didn't think you'd be able to forgive me."

"Do I really strike you as that hard-hearted?"

Her heart melted at those words. "Oh, Sam."

He pressed his mouth against the side of her head. "When my muscles stop screaming at me I'm going to need to make love to you."

"I have painkillers. And a room."

He squeezed her hand. "One more thing. I don't think I've told you I love you, yet."

Yes. Thank you, Sam. It was exactly what she needed to hear. "I love you, too." She let her head sink against his shoulder.

They stood that way for a long time.

Finally, the kids found them. Josh looked excited. "We checked the official times and guess what? It looks like you qualified for Boston...."

"Another marathon?" Leigh didn't know whether to laugh or cry. Perhaps in a few weeks, when her body had recovered, Boston might seem more appealing.

But right now, all she wanted was to be in Sam's arms. Even as she had the thought, she felt his hand on her tighten.

He put his mouth to her ear. "I want to marry you, Leigh."

On the lake, a motorboat pulled a teenager on a wakeboard.

She thought about Drew and wondered what he would make of these latest developments. His son and their daughter, in the same family at last.

Would it feel as right to him as it did to her?

"Leigh?"

"Yes, Sam. I want that, too."

* * * * *

Award-winning author Stevi Mittman
delivers another hysterical mystery, featur-
ing Teddi Bayer, an irrepressible heroine,
and her to-die-for hero, Detective Drew
Scoones. After all, life on Long Island can
be murder!

*Turn the page for a sneak peek at the warm
and funny fourth book,
WHOSE NUMBER IS UP, ANYWAY?,
in the Teddi Bayer series,
by STEVI MITTMAN.
On sale August 7*

CHAPTER 1

"Before redecorating a room, I always advise my clients to empty it of everything but one chair. Then I suggest they move that chair from place to place, sitting in it, until the placement feels right. Trust your instincts when deciding on furniture placement. Your room should 'feel right.'"

—TipsFromTeddi.com

Gut feelings. You know, that gnawing in the pit of your stomach that warns you that you are about to do the absolute stupidest thing you could do? Something that will ruin life as you know it?

I've got one now, standing at the butcher counter in King Kullen, the grocery store in the same strip mall as L.I. Lanes, the bowling alley-cum-billiard parlor I'm in the process of redecorating for its "Grand Opening."

I realize being in the wrong supermarket

probably doesn't sound exactly dire to you, but you aren't the one buying your father a brisket at a store your mother will somehow know isn't Waldbaum's.

And then, June Bayer isn't your mother.

The woman behind the counter has agreed to go into the freezer to find a brisket for me, since there aren't any in the case. There are packages of pork tenderloin, piles of spareribs and rolls of sausage, but no briskets.

Warning Number Two, right? I should be so out of here.

But no, I'm still in the same spot when she comes back out, brisketless, her face ashen. She opens her mouth as if she is going to scream, but only a gurgle comes out.

And then she pinballs out from behind the counter, knocking bottles of Peter Luger Steak Sauce to the floor on her way, now hitting the tower of cans at the end of the prepared foods aisle and sending them sprawling, now making her way down the aisle, careening from side to side as she goes.

Finally, from a distance, I hear her shout, "He's deeeeeeaaaad! Joey's deeeeeaaaad."

My first thought is, *You should always trust your gut.*

My second thought is that now, somehow, my mother will know I was in King Kullen. For weeks I will have to hear "What did you expect?" as though whenever you go to King Kullen someone turns up dead. And if the detective investigating the case turns out to be Detective Drew Scoones …well, I'll never hear the end of that from her, either.

She still suspects I murdered the guy who was found dead on my doorstep last Halloween just to get Drew back into my life.

Several people head for the butcher's freezer and I position myself to block them. If there's one thing I've learned from finding people dead— and the guy on my doorstep wasn't the first one— it's that the police get very testy when you mess with their murder scenes.

"You can't go in there until the police get here," I say, stationing myself at the end of the butcher's counter and in front of the Employees Only door, acting as if I'm some sort of authority. "You'll contaminate the evidence if it turns out to be murder."

Shouts and chaos. You'd think I'd know better than to throw the word *murder* around. Cell phones are flipping open and tongues are wagging.

I amend my statement quickly. "Which, of course, it probably isn't. Murder, I mean. People die all the time, and it's not always in hospitals or their own beds, or…" I babble when I'm nervous, and the idea of someone dead on the other side of the freezer door makes me very nervous.

So does the idea of seeing Drew Scoones again. Drew and I have this on-again, off-again sort of thing…that I kind of turned off.

Who knew he'd take it so personally when he tried to get serious and I responded by saying we could talk about *us* tomorrow—and then caught a plane to my parents' condo in Boca the next day? In July. In the middle of a job.

For some crazy reason, he took that to mean that I was avoiding him and the subject of *us*.

That was three months ago. I haven't seen him since.

The manager, who identifies himself and points to his nameplate in case I don't believe him, says he has to go into *his cooler.* "Maybe Joey's not dead," he says. "Maybe he can be saved, and you're letting him die in there. Did you ever think of that?"

In fact, I hadn't. But I had thought that the murderer might try to go back in to make sure his tracks were covered, so I say that I will go in and check.

Which means that the manager and I couple up and go in together while everyone pushes against the doorway to peer in, erasing any chance of finding clean prints on that Employees Only door.

I expect to find carcasses of dead animals hanging from hooks, and maybe Joey hanging from one, too. I think it's going to be very creepy and I steel myself, only to find a rather benign series of shelves with large slabs of meat laid out carefully on them, along with boxes and boxes marked simply Chicken.

Nothing scary here, unless you count the body of a middle-aged man with graying hair sprawled faceup on the floor. His eyes are wide open and unblinking. His shirt is stiff. His pants are stiff. His body is stiff. And his expression, you should forgive the pun—is frozen. Bill-the-manager crosses himself and stands mute while I pronounce the guy dead in a sort of *happy now?* tone.

"We should not be in here," I say, and he nods his head emphatically and helps me push people out of the doorway just in time to hear the police sirens and see the cop cars pull up outside the big store windows.

Bobbie Lyons, my partner in Teddi Bayer Interior Designs (and also my neighbor, my best friend and my private fashion police), and Mark, our carpenter (and my dogsitter, confidant and ego booster), rush in from next door. They beat the cops by a half step and shout out my name. People point in my direction.

After all the publicity that followed the unfortunate incident during which I shot my ex-husband, Rio Gallo, and then the subsequent murder of my first client—which I solved, I might add—it seems like the whole world, or at least all of Long Island, knows who I am.

Mark asks if I'm all right. (Did I remember to mention that the man is drop-dead-gorgeous-but-a-decade-too-young-for-me-yet-too-old-for-my-daughter-thank-god?) I don't get a chance to answer him because the police are quickly closing in on the store manager and me.

"The woman—" I begin telling the police. Then I have to pause for the manager to fill in her name, which he does: *Fran.*

I continue. "Right. Fran. Fran went into the freezer to get a brisket. A moment later she came out and screamed that Joey was dead. So I'd say she was the one who discovered the body."

"And you are…?" the cop asks me. It comes out a bit like who do I *think* I am, rather than who am I really?

"An innocent bystander," Bobbie, hair perfect,

makeup just right, says, carefully placing her body between the cop and me.

"And she was just leaving," Mark adds. They each take one of my arms.

Fran comes into the inner circle surrounding the cops. In case it isn't obvious from the hairnet and bloodstained white apron with Fran embroidered on it, I explain that she was the butcher who was going for the brisket. Mark and Bobbie take that as a signal that I've done my job and they can now get me out of there. They twist around, with me in the middle, as if we're a Rockettes line, until we are facing away from the butcher counter. They've managed to propel me a few steps toward the exit when disaster—in the form of a Mazda RX7 pulling up at the loading curb—strikes.

Mark's grip on my arm tightens like a vise. "Too late," he says.

Bobbie's expletive is unprintable. "Maybe there's a back door," she suggests, but Mark is right. It's too late.

I've laid my eyes on Detective Scoones. And while my gut is trying to warn me that my heart shouldn't go there, regions farther south are melting at just the sight of him.

"Walk," Bobbie orders me.

And I try to. Really.

Walk, I tell my feet. *Just put one foot in front of the other.*

I can do this because I know, in my heart of hearts, that if Drew Scoones was still interested in me, he'd have gotten in touch with me after I returned from Boca. And he didn't.

Since he's a detective, Drew doesn't have to wear one of those dark blue Nassau County Police uniforms. Instead, he's got on jeans, a tight-fitting T-shirt and a tweedy sports jacket. If you think that sounds good, you should see him. Chiseled features, cleft chin, brown hair that's naturally a little sandy in the front, a smile that…well, that doesn't matter. He isn't smiling now.

He walks up to me, tucks his sunglasses into his breast pocket and looks me over from head to toe.

"Well, if it isn't Miss Cut and Run," he says. "Aren't you supposed to be somewhere in Florida or something?" He looks at Mark accusingly, as if he was covering for me when he told Drew I was gone.

"Detective Scoones?" one of the uniforms says. "The stiff's in the cooler and the woman who found him is over there." He jerks his head in Fran's direction.

Drew continues to stare at me.

You know how when you were young, your mother always told you to wear clean underwear in case you were in an accident? And how, a little farther on, she told you not to go out in hair rollers because you never knew who you might see—or who might see you? And how now your best friend says she wouldn't be caught dead without makeup and suggests you shouldn't, either?

Okay, today, *finally,* in my overalls and Converse sneakers, I get it.

I brush my hair out of my eyes. "Well, I'm back," I say. As if he hasn't known my exact whereabouts. The man is a detective, for heaven's sake. "Been back awhile."

Bobbie has watched the exchange and apparently decided she's given Drew all the time he deserves. "And we've got work to do, so…" she says, grabbing my arm and giving Drew a little two-fingered wave goodbye.

As I back up a foot or two, the store manager sees his chance and places himself in front of Drew, trying to get his attention. Maybe what makes Drew such a good detective is his ability to focus.

Only what he's focusing on is me.

"Phone broken? Carrier pigeon died?" he asks

me, taking in Fran, the manager, the meat counter and that Employees Only door, all without taking his eyes off me.

Mark tries to break the spell. "We've got work to do there, you've got work to do here, Scoones," Mark says to him, gesturing toward next door. "So it's back to the alley for us."

Drew's lip twitches. "You working the alley now?" he says.

"If you'd like to follow me," Bill-the-manager, clearly exasperated, says to Drew—who doesn't respond. It's as if waiting for my answer is all he has to do.

So, fine. "You knew I was back," I say.

The man has known my whereabouts every hour of the day for as long as I've known him. And my mother's not the only one who won't buy that he "just happened" to answer this particular call. In fact, I'm willing to bet my children's lunch money that he's taken every call within ten miles of my home since the day I got back.

And now he's gotten lucky.

"*You* could have called *me*," I say.

"You're the one who said *tomorrow* for our talk and then flew the coop, chickie," he says. "I figured the ball was in your court."

"Detective?" the uniform says. "There's something you ought to see in here."

Drew gives me a look that amounts to *in or out?*

He could be talking about the investigation, or about our relationship.

Bobbie tries to steer me away. Mark's fists are balled. Drew waits me out, knowing I won't be able to resist what might be a murder investigation.

Finally he turns and heads for the cooler.

And, like a puppy dog, I follow.

Bobbie grabs the back of my shirt and pulls me to a halt.

"I'm just going to show him something," I say, yanking away.

"Yeah," Bobbie says, pointedly looking at the buttons on my blouse. The two at breast level have popped. "That's what I'm afraid of."

HARLEQUIN®

Super Romance®

*Looking for a romantic, emotional
and unforgettable escape?*

*You'll find it this month and every month
with a Harlequin Superromance!*

Rory Gorenzi has a sense of humor and a sense of
honor. She also happens to be good with children.

Seamus Lee, widower and father of four, needs
someone with exactly those traits.

They meet at the Colorado mountain school owned
by Rory's father, where she teaches skiing and
avalanche safety. But Seamus—and his children—
learn more from her than that....

Look for

GOOD WITH CHILDREN

by Margot Early,

*available August 2007, and these other
fantastic titles from Harlequin Superromance.*

REQUEST YOUR FREE BOOKS!
2 FREE NOVELS PLUS 2 FREE GIFTS!

HARLEQUIN®

Super Romance®

Exciting, emotional, unexpected!

YES! Please send me 2 FREE Harlequin Superromance® novels and my 2 FREE gifts. After receiving them, if I don't wish to receive any more books, I can return the shipping statement marked "cancel." If I don't cancel, I will receive 6 brand-new novels every month and be billed just $4.69 per book in the U.S., or $5.24 per book in Canada, plus 25¢ shipping and handling per book and applicable taxes, if any*. That's a savings of close to 15% off the cover price! I understand that accepting the 2 free books and gifts places me under no obligation to buy anything. I can always return a shipment and cancel at any time. Even if I never buy another book from Harlequin, the two free books and gifts are mine to keep forever.   135 HDN EEX7 336 HDN EEYK

Name	(PLEASE PRINT)	
Address		Apt.
City	State/Prov.	Zip/Postal Code

Signature (if under 18, a parent or guardian must sign)

Mail to the **Harlequin Reader Service®:**
IN U.S.A.: P.O. Box 1867, Buffalo, NY 14240-1867
IN CANADA: P.O. Box 609, Fort Erie, Ontario L2A 5X3

Not valid to current Harlequin Superromance subscribers.

Want to try two free books from another line?
Call 1-800-873-8635 or visit www.morefreebooks.com.

* Terms and prices subject to change without notice. NY residents add applicable sales tax. Canadian residents will be charged applicable provincial taxes and GST. This offer is limited to one order per household. All orders subject to approval. Credit or debit balances in a customer's account(s) may be offset by any other outstanding balance owed by or to the customer. Please allow 4 to 6 weeks for delivery.

Your Privacy: Harlequin is committed to protecting your privacy. Our Privacy Policy is available online at www.eHarlequin.com or upon request from the Reader Service. From time to time we make our lists of customers available to reputable firms who may have a product or service of interest to you. If you would prefer we not share your name and address, please check here. ☐

COMING NEXT MONTH

HSRCNM0707